The remaining days of summer collapsed into hours. I tried to savor them, extend them, but each was a final.

Final day sailing.

Final tennis game.

Final movie and popcorn.

I helped Jaz pack. Filled out an address book for him, in case he actually did write letters. I baked him three dozen chocolate chip cookies to take. He and Michael polished them off that afternoon.

The last afternoon.

Before he left.

Before Flavia left.

Before they all left.

Other Point paperbacks you will enjoy:

THE PARTY'S OVER

Caroline B. Cooney

SCHOLASTIC INC.
New York Toronto London Auckland Sydney

No part of this publication may be reproduced in whole or in part, or stored in a retrieval system, or transmitted in any form or by any means, electronic, mechanical, photocopying, recording, or otherwise, without written permission of the publisher. For information regarding permission, write to Scholastic Inc., 730 Broadway, New York, NY 10003.

ISBN 0-590-42553-6

Copyright © 1991 by Caroline B. Cooney.
All rights reserved. Published by Scholastic Inc.
POINT is a registered trademark of Scholastic Inc.

12 11 10 9 8 7 6 5 4 3 2   2 3 4 5 6 7/9

Printed in the U.S.A.   01

One

Everybody loves to swear.
  I know I do.

I started swearing in seventh grade when I failed an exam. I was completely demoralized, especially because Flavia got her usual 98. I succumbed to temptation and whispered "Damn!" under my breath.

How wild and criminal it sounded! I felt quite a bit older after my first swear; more worldly and sophisticated. Flavia says I even swaggered a bit. Instead of being a total humiliation, the failed exam became something I could (almost) joke about.

Swearing turned out to be a siphon; you turned the valve and let out the bad. (My mother, of course, felt differently. Swearing, Gloria said, turns the valve and lets *in* the bad.)

The years passed. Flavia continued to get 98 in everything, and I continued to swear because I didn't.

My best friends keep their knowledge like a wardrobe, pulling it out, adding to it, accessorizing it. They groom their knowledge the way I groom my hair.

I study, get passing grades, and retain nothing. When the final exam is over, my knowledge vanishes as if I'd never had it. Cumulative subjects, like math, are tricky, since I don't accumulate. One-time subjects, like European history, aren't so bad; I can hang onto a specific war, peace treaty, or river boundary until the tests are over.

However, learning is so far down on my list of interesting activities as to be invisible.

I like to run things. Each year I pick up another activity to run, along with school, and this year I carried Drama Club, the school paper, the Biking Expedition, and Students Against Drunk Driving. All senior year I've been busy with Class Spirit. I wanted our senior year to be not only the most memorable year of our lives, but also the most memorable in the history of high schools. This required effort. My fellow seniors at Westerly High, I regret to report, preferred to lie down, daydream, or doze.

I do not believe in rest. I believe in Spirit.

"There are only forty-seven of us," my class protested last fall. "How much spirit can forty-seven seniors raise?"

"More than this," I insisted, swearing at them. At that time the class-wide hobby was swearing. Delete the swear words and nothing was left. Listening to myself that day, I decided that swearing does not go with Spirit. Maybe turning seventeen made me conservative; who knows. At any rate, I went on a swear diet.

But like being on a team, it's so much easier to exert yourself if somebody else is sweating on each side of you. So I ordered the senior class to go on a swear diet with me. I've stuck to my diet without lapses, but this is one place where I led and nobody followed.

Including my boyfriend.

"Damn," Jaz said, glaring at the platform he was building. "We need two more sheets of plywood. Who measured this, anyway?" He swung his hammer threateningly. Jaz is very thin, very tall, with silky, scalp-colored hair. I tell him nobody will notice when he goes bald. He tells me thank you, Hallie, that's so reassuring. I adore him.

"*I* measured it," I said with dignity.

"Oh, no, we let Hallie the Math Wizard measure something?" Flavia said. Flavia is elegant. Since elementary school she has worn her yellow hair the same way — a man's soccer cut, like a layered bowl. She hasn't grown taller since elementary school, either. There is a timeless element to Flavia; as if, world without end, fashions may change and TV sitcoms go off the air, but Flavia will go on forever, being smarter, lippier, and more yellow-haired than the rest of us.

"Give me your hammer, Jaz," I said to my boyfriend. "I need to put dents in Flavia."

He laughed and hung on to the hammer. "Forgot about the diet. Sorry."

"Just because she's on a swear diet doesn't mean we have to be," Flavia said. "I'm so nervous about college I have to swear. Yesterday a letter came about freshman orientation."

Everybody building Athletic Banquet platforms set down their tools. Everybody stuffing purple and white paper flowers into chicken wire stopped making the ten-foot baseball player. (Actually our tallest baseball player is five nine. We don't run to height in this town but for a banquet you need drama.)

Talk turned to college.

The only thing I hold against senior year is the amount of college talk in it. We have had assemblies to discuss choosing colleges, visiting colleges, applying to colleges, paying for colleges. Both the principal and guidance counselor start every speech with "Of course . . ." because *of course* you're going to college. *Of course* you aren't content with a pathetic little high school diploma. *Of course* you understand high school is merely a launching pad for college and not an end in itself.

Kyle discussed Penn State, where his dorm alone would have twelve hundred people. Susannah talked about her plane flight to California, where she was going because her single criterion for college was Distance From Parents. Max repeated what his cousin said about the cost of textbooks.

"You're slipping into a coma," Jaz murmured to me.

"College talk does it every time."

"I wish you'd go to college, too, Hallie. Come with me. I want you."

"Jaz. Drop it." College holds nothing I want. It's full of what I don't want: more studying. Besides, college is so far off. How can you fully enjoy June when you're bogged down worrying about next September?

"Your grades are high enough," Jaz said.

They aren't, actually. I give off an aura of academic success, but there's no reality to it. Even Flavia and Jaz, who know me, have seen my report cards, and looked at my quizzes, are taken in by the aura and think I'm intelligent. It's rather nice to go through life sounding as if I know what I'm talking about. Spares me the trouble of actually learning anything. "Maybe so, Jaz, but my interest is zero."

It makes me nervous, the way my friends are so obsessed with college. On the other hand, it probably makes them nervous the way I'm so obsessed with Jaz.

Jaz's parents decided to spend the winter at their summer home this year and expected him to stay gracefully at boarding school. He refused, flew to Maine, and entered Westerly High. Mr. and Mrs. Innes were appalled. Their only child was not only attending a "local" school, but graduating from it, thus forever staining his name. They use the word "local" as other people might use the word "sewers." They are genuinely surprised that Jaz got into a top college in spite of this. They insist it's only because three of his four high school years were at a prep school, and the colleges "overlooked" a senior year in a "local" school. I need hardly say Mr. and Mrs. Innes are not my favorite people. However, they are Jaz's favorite people, so I watch myself.

At the time Jaz entered Westerly High, we were having yearbook elections for Best Liked, Best Dressed, Most Likely to Succeed, and so forth, all of which I intended to be. Flavia said I just smiled at the new boy because he was a vote. (This was not the case; I had no competition.) No, Jasper Innes walked into my English class, and I knew this was a boy I could study for hours. Months. Possibly years. I felt a literal wave of interest in him, like surfing.

Obsession is an interesting thing. It's time-consuming, portable, invisible . . . and taboo.

Intensity terrifies people.

I think about Jaz all the time, in all ways. "Demented," people would say if they knew. "You need counseling, Hallie. You have difficulty with normal human relationships."

The only two acceptable obsessions, at least here in Maine, are sports and cars. If a boy got up at dawn, and spent hours lifting weights, swimming laps, and shooting baskets, people would say respectfully, "Do you know he works out for two hours before school every day?" Or if a girl sacrificed everything, never so much as bought a Coke, to save for a new truck, people would be in awe of her. "She's so determined," they'd say, impressed.

But look at Brittany, who is obsessed with knitting and is always sitting in the back row of class, needles clicking, yarn pouring off her lap. Never mind that she has the most beautiful sweaters on earth. "So pathetic," everybody says behind her back. "Like an old lady." Or Kyle, who sings madrigals. When I was organizing the Biking Expedition and being Editor of the yearbook, Kyle was starting up a madrigal choir, which sings the most anorexic, undernourished little songs you've ever heard. "Such a geek," they whisper behind Kyle's back.

Love is not sports or cars. It is not a valid obsession. If people knew how much I love Jaz, they would want me to love him *less*. They'd slot love right in there with knitting and madrigals. ("Weird kid, that Hallie Revness, obsessed with Jaz. It's sick, isn't it? I feel sorry for her parents.")

So people don't know. They think it's just a high school romance.

Jaz separated out some strands of my hair (I have armloads of long, thick, wavy black hair) and tied them under my chin like a bonnet. "I still say you should consider college, Hallie."

"Shut up about college, Jaz," I said. "I'm on a swear diet and I don't want to break it."

"You'll write me a million letters, won't you, Hallie?"

"No, but I'll make a million phone calls."

I'm always phoning Jaz. His mother usually answers. Mrs. Innes breathes slowly, calming herself before calling Jaz to the phone. Mr. and Mrs. Innes are not happy that Jaz is in love with me, and they certainly never refer to it as love. (Whenever I show up, they act startled, as if they had not expected a return performance. "Oh, are you going on another date?" Or, "Why, hello, uh — Hallie.")

College talk went on around me.

I molded chicken wire around a basketball. I ran curving rows of purple paper flowers around the form, to represent the stitching, and filled in the rest with white. Then I wired it to the hand of my ten-foot baseball player. Westerly High won the States this year, can you believe that? A school this small? First time in eighteen years!

"I don't want to be unsophisticated," Flavia said. "I'm worried about my clothes and my shoes and my accent."

Flavia and I have been best friends since birth, sharing everything from tennis lessons to peanut butter-and-Fluff sandwiches. (We used to call them PB and F, leaning heavily on the F, which back in elementary school was the closest we ever came to swearing. "Well, Fluff you!" we'd insult each other.) It irritates me that she worries about measuring up. "Fluff off," I muttered in her direction.

"At Princeton," Flavia said, "every single freshman will have been number one in high school. I'll be *average*. I'll *blend in*. Nobody will know me or notice me."

"Oh, no!" said a voice dramatically. "She'll be *average*! Oh, poor baby." The voice went thick with anger. "You're not worried about being average, Flavia. You just want to say out loud one more time about how *you're* going to *Princeton*."

I was a little surprised to see Johnny D'Andrea in school this early in the morning. My crew was here to prepare the Athletic Banquet, but even though Johnny was captain of our winning baseball team, he has no school spirit at all, will not join things, will not work on things, and certainly will not arrive inside the building one minute before he has to.

Johnny is a true local, the kind Mr. and Mrs. Innes worry might infect Jaz. Mr. D'Andrea manages a marina, and Johnny, who loves motors, has been getting his fingers oil-stained with repairs since grade school. There's nothing wrong with Johnny, exactly, except that he's ordinary.

It's enough.

Our senior year is the total eclipse. His is plain old noonday.

I stuffed a few more flowers in my "baseball," keeping busy. I pretty much feel this is *my* senior class: I created it, I'm in charge of it, and I'm responsible for it. I like us to be a forty-seven-member family, with no cliques, and I hate evidence to the contrary.

Flavia put her hands on her hips, swung around to show Johnny D'Andrea her back, and surveyed our ten-foot baseball player. "Hallie, what is that huge tube?"

"Baseball bat."

"Six feet long?"

"We need drama. I want my centerpiece to be the best ever. Center front and newsworthy."

"You want center front, Hallie?" Johnny said. "What a surprise."

Sarcasm should be outlawed. The only thing it ever does is make a person be sarcastic back, till everybody's spitting at everybody else.

I handed over a box of doughnuts that still had some good ones in it, chocolate covered or jelly filled. "Be a sport, Johnny. This flower man is for you. In fact, he *is* you. I'm even going to put the cap backward in your honor."

Johnny never wears his baseball cap frontward, but jams it down backward with such vigor that his forehead has added a crease. A short, eighteen-year-old Italian muscleman with a fifty-year-old forehead. *Johnny, Johnny, he's our man, if he can't do it, nobody can.* "Did you drive your truck to school, Johnny?" I asked. "Would you take Jaz and get two more sheets of plywood?"

Johnny was not interested in doing any favors for the rich kid. "Whatsamatter? Can't fit plywood into your Jaguar?" said Johnny to Jaz.

Can you imagine a high school senior driving a Jaguar to school every day? In a village where every kid is driving a rusted-out hundred thousand miler or a fourth-hand pickup truck, that sleek metallic gray Jag with its red leather interior is pretty noticeable.

How I love that car. His Jaguar is our private world. Our party; our phone booth; our hideout. The horn is sharp and piercing; Jaz beeps my initial in Morse code whenever he sees me, thinks of me, or drives past my house. H is *dit*, *dit*, *dit*, *dit*. Nobody in this graduating class will ever forget H.

"Sure," Jaz said, "we can carry four-by-eights in the Jag. My father won't notice if we knock out the windows."

I thought it was funny, but Johnny took it literally: a father with so much money that a destroyed English sports car would be beneath his notice.

I have a lot of charm; I really do. It even works with a Johnny D'Andrea. I love being charming. I plan to conquer the world with it, which annoys Flavia. She plans to conquer the world, too, but she has a different one in mind. She wants to be a President of a Fortune 500 corporation, or else Ambassador to Moscow. She's always talking about getting her master's degree. Without an MBA, she likes to tell me scornfully, you might as well be a hairdresser.

So I charmed Johnny, who agreed to take Jaz in his truck and charge more plywood at the lumberyard. Jaz was grinning; he knew exactly what I was doing. But then, so did Johnny. Johnny fished in his jacket pocket for his keys. "How are you two lovebirds going to survive college?" he said. "You'll be a thousand miles apart come September."

"Mid-August, actually," corrected Jaz. "Orientation. Seventy-seven days till I leave."

"Eighty-one for me," said Michael.

"Seventy-eight for me," called Susannah.

I could not believe what I was hearing. We had the rest of senior year still to go! The best was yet to come — Senior Prom! "You worked out countdowns?" I said.

"Of course," Flavia said. "College is the most important thing on earth. You have to know when you're going."

Fluff off! College is not the most important thing on earth! "You're not going for ages," I protested. "We haven't even graduated. There's all summer yet. The beach. Sailing. Tennis. Going out to the islands."

"You make it sound like a thousand years of sun and sand," Jaz teased. He pulled my hair. "Come with us to the lumberyard."

"Too much to do," I said. "If I'm not here, this bunch will fade. Sit around and eat jelly doughnuts or something."

Michael waved his index card. (I write out people's assignments; otherwise they manage to forget their fair share.) "Nine chores on my list alone," he said, grinning. "I feel as if I'm going to graduate from Hallie instead of high school. I think I date Flavia just to have somebody standing between me and Hallie."

Our class took up kissing at about the time I ordered the swear diet. We kiss for everything, as though agreement and laughter can be sealed only by lips. We kiss hello and good-bye, kiss good luck before exams, kiss congratulations on awards.

Michael gave me a kiss: enjoying how I organize us all — cheek location.

Johnny gave me a kiss: apologizing — forehead location.

Jaz gave me a kiss: in love — lip location. (Greater duration than the previous two; round of applause from bystanders.)

I surveyed my Athletic Banquet, my purple-flowered baseball player, and my graduating classmates.

The world was perfect. I owned it, I ran it, and it was mine.

TWO

"Hallie Revness to the principal's office," said the loudspeaker.

"Hallie, you take up crime?" the boys asked me.

I was already on my feet, laughing, hugging myself. "No. I think the yearbooks are here."

The class went berserk. "Run! Bring ours first! Want help?"

Ever since my brothers graduated (barely) I have dreamed about my yearbook. My brothers were too busy getting in trouble even to get their yearbooks signed. Can you imagine that? A bare, naked, unwritten-in yearbook?

Other than Jaz, nothing in my life has been more fun than being Editor of the yearbook.

I tore down the hall. (Flavia would never have run; it would look too eager, and Flavia never wants to look too anything.) I flung open the office door, yelled hello to the secretaries (friends of my mother's; my mother has worked everywhere and knows everybody), and ran into Dr. Stefford's office.

Dr. Stefford is one of my fans. He remembered my brothers and did not expect much from me, except detentions and suspensions. He says meeting a third Revness awakened his interest in genes. How can the same family produce two complete losers and one complete winner? "They're here, Hallie, and they're beautiful. We've never had a better one. This yearbook will definitely win the state award."

I picked up a yearbook. How beautifully the cover had turned out! Dark purple leather with embossed white letters in arched script. I ran a cover design contest, which was won, annoyingly enough, by Marcy Hampson, who moved here from Louisiana and hates Maine. Nobody has bothered to be friends with Marcy. She has nothing going for her except, supposedly, she's headed back to Louisiana.

Earlier yearbooks I studied, like my brothers', were crammed with photographs — no blank space for writing messages. My design included plenty of writing room. I love writing notes to people in their yearbook, and Westerly High is so small, you always know the entire graduating class, even when you're a freshman. Writing yearbook farewells is big business at Westerly High.

Title page: Perfect.

Graduates list: No misspellings.

Teacher photographs, club photographs, lower-class group pictures: Captions correct.

Only one page really counted. I turned to the

carefully posed "candids" over which I had labored so many hours.

> Class Leader . . . Hallie
> Most Brilliant . . . Flavia
> Most Style . . . Jaz
> Best Dressed . . . Hallie
> Most Spirit . . . Hallie
> Class Couple . . . Hallie and Jaz

My black hair, his blue eyes. His six foot three, my five foot six. In the picture I had chosen, I was looking at the camera, my obsession carefully hidden, but Jaz was looking down at me, his obsession hidden not at all.

Hot fierce pleasure filled me. I had gotten everything I wanted from senior year; if it didn't come to me, I worked and fought till I earned it. I turned the page as if it didn't matter, as if it were routine. But the page trembled as it settled.

Forever and ever, no matter where we are or what we are doing, when the forty-seven graduates of Westerly High look at their yearbooks, Jaz and I will be Class Couple.

Actually, there are only forty-six. Orrin dropped out in March. It was April before anyone noticed. "Where's Orrin?" somebody asked one day. We looked around the cafeteria, as if Orrin might be eating his tuna casserole under the table. Everybody else was laughing, but I felt terrible that nobody had missed Orrin. "Don't let me end up like Orrin," I kept saying to people, "weeks passing before any-body spots I'm missing."

"You? The high priestess of telephones?" Flavia said. "If we didn't notice you were missing, you'd call up to tell us."

True. I spend a great deal of time lying on my bed, listening to the radio, and telephoning every-body I know in rotation. I have a love affair with Jaz's car phone as well as with Jaz. It helps to have flawless phone number memory. I know my grad-uating class by their telephone numbers. Or at least, my crowd. I didn't know Orrin's number. Who would call him? I would have to find him and get his year-book to him; he had paid for it.

"May I distribute them now, Dr. Stefford? Please?"

He wouldn't refuse. Nobody refuses me. Sure enough, the principal laughed, shrugged, and helped me set up shop in the corridor. Passing bells rang, and I had to fend off juniors, sophomores, and freshmen who wanted theirs now, too. "I paid," they cried. "No fair, Hallie. Let us have ours, too!"

"Forget it. Seniors first." I love saying that: I'm a senior; I'm first.

Kyle took his yearbook and kissed me.

I handed a yearbook to Marcy. She's rabbit-y look-ing, with a mouth that doesn't open wide enough for her face, just makes a little pink hole.

In elementary school, Flavia and I were the girls everybody wanted to be with. My mother was always ordering us to be friendly to creeps like Marcy who attached themselves to us. We tried, but all we ever were was "friend-ish" — faking friendliness. "Lovely cover," I said friend-ishly. "Thank you for doing it so well, Marcy."

"Uh-huh," said Marcy, not even attempting to be friend-ish. She took the yearbook and walked away.

Susannah took hers, shrieking, "Are the candids good, Hallie? Did you put in lots of me? I want to be plastered all over the place." She turned to the back and screamed again. "Oooooh, look at me! Me in the senior play. Me as majorette. Me as — Hallie, you creep. You have me falling down the time there was ice on the parade ground."

"But you fell so gracefully. You had to be immortalized that way."

Johnny D'Andrea reached for his yearbook.

"Great candids of you in the sports section," I told him.

Johnny simply nodded. Took his yearbook and walked on without opening it, talking to some sophomore who works in his father's marina. As if boats, of which there are millions, matter more than our yearbook, of which there is one!

"Do we have to go to class, Dr. Stefford?" the seniors cried. "Can this be Senior Skip Hour?"

"There's no such thing," said the principal. "Go to class."

Jaz came up behind me and pressed against my back, toasting me. Boys are so much hotter than girls. When my brothers still lived at home, Mom used to say, "Turn off the furnace — the boys are here."

"You're my favorite furnace, Jaz," I whispered. I wanted him to go crazy when he saw our pictures in the yearbook. I admit there are more of the two of us than of anybody, but I did the most work, so I got to choose. That's fair.

"Seniors," the principal said, "have exactly one minute to get to their next class or suffer the consequences."

"Oh, no, anything but that!" We giggled insanely. "Consequences! Dr. Stefford, we're in your hands only seventeen more days. What consequences?"

"You guys count weekends? In actual fact, you're in my hands ten more days. Today doesn't count," said Dr. Stefford. "Prom weekend, five days of class, another weekend, five days of class, graduation on Sunday."

I was truly shocked. *Ten days?* Where could senior year have gone? It made me cold and heavy. I normally dance at all times, in all places. I like to think of the high school corridor as a long narrow stage just for me. Ten days and high school would be over?

"The only thing you missed is Most Brilliant, Hallie," said Jaz. "So what was the problem?" He was laughing. He grabbed a hank of my hair and made himself a mustache. I have a great deal of hair. If I wear it loose, it takes up so much room that Flavia refers to it as my parasol. If I braid it in various intricate arrangements, Jaz sits behind me in class and unbraids it.

I never respond to remarks about brainpower, any

more than Jaz responds to remarks about rich kid/ summer person. The best way to deal with difficult topics is not to deal with them. "The next thing we need to be," I told Jaz, "is Prom King and Queen."

"Not to worry. I've been paying off the voters. I think I've bagged it." He ran all ten fingers into my hair, letting his yearbook fall to the floor. Dividing my hair like drapes, he kissed my forehead.

I said, "You damaged your yearbook, letting go of it like that."

"Yeah, well, you damaged my heart. Fair's fair."

After school, everybody met in the parking lot, leaning on Jaz's Jaguar. You know who's "in" by who gathers around the Jag. Now that sports are over and clubs have had their last meeting, it's an endless party. I can hardly wait for summer; we'll party around the clock.

"We could go to my house," Jaz suggested.

"Your parents yelled at us last time because we made too much noise and they were working," Michael said. Michael hates being yelled at, which is a hardship for a jock; coaches do nothing but yell at you.

"McDonald's?" I said. We have a very small town. It supports only one fast-food place; for more you have to drive sixty miles south to Sable Mall. But the boys won't go; they don't like shopping.

"Not McDonald's," said Flavia. "Everybody else will be there."

Johnny D'Andrea swung past, headed to his truck.

"God forbid, Flavia, that you should be forced to associate with *everybody*." He slammed his truck door, like a child; revved his motor, like a kid; and when he zoomed off, left a patch, like a delinquent. We rolled our eyes.

"Let's go to Sea Storm and order Cokes," Flavia said.

Sea Storm is an expensive resort. They specialize in Weekends: Murder Mystery Weekends, Famous French Chef Weekends, Cross-Country Ski Weekends. My mother has done Fitness Weekends. Fitness is Gloria's religion: something to do frequently, seriously, and devotedly. People who are Unfit, Smoke, or Abuse Their Bodies, are sinning. My mother is forty-five and has the figure of an Olympic medalist. People are very tired when they wrap up one of her Fitness Weekends. It's tiring to live with Gloria, too. The only time I can catch her is when she's on her exercise bike and then I have to shout over the clicking of the stationary miles.

Sea Storm is formal. Waiters wear tuxedos; waitresses, white lace aprons over black dresses. Dark rich colors cover the walls, and thick rich carpets blanket the floors. Needless to say, they dislike teenagers dropping in after school to use Sea Storm like a hamburger joint. I am the one who started that hobby. The first day we went, we brought our own tea bags and ordered hot water. They would have thrown us out, but my mother was helping in the kitchen at the time, and they were desperate, so they put up with us.

Jaz tired of the discussion and lowered himself into the driver's seat, passing the time by honking H for Hallie. Everybody yelled *dit, dit, dit, dit* along with him.

"I'll always think of you like that, Hallie," said Marcy Hampson, walking to her rusted-out piece of junk car. "A *dit, dit, dit, dit*."

To think I had even bothered being friend-ish.

"We have to graduate with that," muttered Flavia.

"It's okay," Marcy called back. "Nobody at Princeton will know, Flavia. You're safe."

I was sick of waiting for a consensus. Anyway, I hate group decisions. I like to make decisions myself. "The hot dog stand at West Beach just opened for the season," I informed the group. "We'll meet there."

I got in the car with Jaz. Marcy Hampson made a big deal of waving the Jaguar ahead of her, bowing over her steering wheel.

I wanted to talk about my yearbook. I stroked the cover, pretending somebody other than Marcy Hampson had designed it.

"Seventy-seven days," Jaz said. "Hard to believe, isn't it? I think about college all the time, no matter what else I'm doing." He held his breath, a new habit that went only with college conversations: as though he froze his lungs in order to daydream.

You think about college more than me?

"Applications were scary, but now that it's settled, and I'm going to Ann Arbor, I can't wait." Jaz drove contentedly, as if going to college left no holes; it was complete unto itself.

You call some colleges by town instead of by name. If you're going to the University of North Carolina, you call it Chapel Hill; if you're going to Yale, you call it New Haven; and if, like Jaz, you're going to the University of Michigan, you call it Ann Arbor. I know the college lingo, too, now; but it makes me lonely to hear it. It's their lingo, not mine.

"You know what?" Jaz said. "Michael, Flavia, Kyle, Susannah, and I leave within a week of each other for freshman orientation." Savoring the phrase like a hard candy on his tongue, he repeated, "Mid-August."

"We'll throw one good-bye party after another," I said.

"What? Oh, yeah," he agreed absently, heart and mind in Ann Arbor.

I could not stand having his attention divided. Seat belts, which Jaz insists on, kept us from sitting thigh to thigh, so I lay down, putting my head on his knee. My hair hung down, filling the space between the steering wheel and the pedals. In warm weather (Jaz and I have shared little of that) Jaz omits socks. I stroked his ankles.

"Hey. You want me to drive off the road?" Jaz said.

"Sure."

Jaz held in laughter. "Lots of traffic. Can't take my hands off the wheel."

I rolled over to look into his face. He took one hand off the wheel anyway and cupped my cheek, and sighed.

Even with layers of tape and cotton, his class ring is too huge for my finger. I wear the ring on a silver necklace. I slid his fourth finger into the ring, chaining us together.

Three

My father watches The News. This is not a matter of glancing toward the television, vaguely registering the story of the day.

He is up at dawn, coffee perked, mug in hand, squatting before the *Early Bird News*. Lunch hour revolves around *Noon Update*. Between five and seven P.M. we keep a reverent silence for local and national evening news, and he would never go to bed before *Nightline*. He also reads two daily papers. Cover to cover.

My father knows oil prices, high fashions, and football. He's up to date on all revolutions, earthquakes, and trends in crime. From Lithuania to Nicaragua, from Israel's borders to Supreme Court decisions, Dennis Revness is there.

But the real world — our town, our family — remains unwitnessed. Dennis knows less about me than about the expansion of Japanese banks. Less about my brothers Royce and Derek than nationalism in Eastern Europe. He was amazed, for example, when Derek divorced Gretchen. Although the process was lengthy, left Gretchen in pain and Derek penniless, my father never noticed anything amiss.

Royce and Derek took the stuffing out of my parents. My brothers were always in trouble. School trouble, girl trouble, drug trouble, car trouble. Royce got speeding tickets. Derek had good clean fun knocking down mailboxes. If Royce shaped up and made basketball team, Derek and his scummy friends crossed the state line and went into bars with fake IDs. If Derek behaved for a marking period, the basketball coach kicked Royce off the team for speeding with drugs instead of cars.

I adored my brothers who, if nothing else, certainly contributed excitement. Life was noisy. The house overflowed with boys, sweat suits, and car repair manuals. (Not schoolbooks; "I did my homework in study hall," Royce and Derek always insisted.)

Gloria, determined to maintain some kind of control (the women in my family are very controlling), took away their cars. I spent my first ten years literally in the backseat, while my mother chauffeured Royce and Derek to work, ball games, girlfriends, and later, to court.

When the boys finally got their high school diplomas, Gloria could hardly wait to get them out of the house. With Derek and Royce, eighteen years had been enough. For Gloria, it was enough of kids, period. "Think you can graduate next year, Helen

Miranda?" my mother said to me. (Helen Miranda is my real name.)

She was not joking. I was ten years old and she was done mothering.

She began the whirlwind of activities that earned her the nickname "Hurricane Gloria." She tends to hold several part-time jobs, which she keeps a while and then rotates on. She clerks at the Sunday Sailor boutique, bakes muffins for the Coffee Shop, does taxes for the Garden Center. She's on the Elderly Housing Committee, takes minutes for the Zoning Board. Her Garden Club plants geraniums in the tubs that line the village sidewalk, and she's a substitute delivery driver for United Parcel.

When I was little, my mother left lists on the refrigerator:

9 to 12, sewing sails
12 till 5, Gale's sick, I'm filling in for her at the
    restaurant
7 to 10, helping with admissions at the Emergency
    Clinic
Love, Mommy

There are no more lists. Gloria says seventeen is too old for lists. I don't agree. It's lonely not knowing where your mother is, or what she's doing. That's the nice thing about school. Five days a week you know exactly where everybody is, what they're doing, and what they're wearing.

I wouldn't mind being cuddled and coddled, but

27

in my family, we grow up, and that's that.

Whereas Flavia's family is a wreck. Princeton is far away. Flavia might miss them; they'll certainly miss her. Mrs. Land bought Flavia a new teddy bear, for absentee hugging. Mr. Land bought her a thick bathrobe, for warmth away from home. College requires so many possessions. If they aren't buying Flavia new sheets, it's a new clock radio, soap dish, or trunk.

I can't remember when my parents last bought me something. I'm expected to decide what I need and get it myself. I have a lot of charge cards. They're not as much fun as you would think.

Hurricane Gloria took up Fitness as her religion; Royce and Derek got apartments, wives, and children; Flavia and I became inseparable. We were always playing cards: week-long games of War. We devoured the *Little House on the Prairie* books and alternated being Laura (adventuresome and worthy) and Mary (blind follower and boring). We took up tennis and sailing and softball. We played flute and got our first two-piece bathing suits. The only real division between us started in seventh grade. I began cheerleading; Flavia began worrying about getting into college. I didn't even know what college was.

In his mid-twenties, Royce made a U-turn into middle-class respectability. He did things like invest carefully and worry about the strength of the carseats bought for his own two little boys.

Derek, however, did not catch on to the whole respectability angle.

I was on Gretchen's side in the divorce. It would have been better to keep Gretchen than Derek. "At least Gretchen can earn a living," I argued. "What can Derek do?" Derek hadn't done anything yet except lose his driver's license — or his temper with the police officers who stopped him.

"He's your brother," my parents said wearily.

Losing Gretchen was a divorce for us all, especially since Gretchen has custody of Meg. Far from fighting for custody, Derek's big worry was that he'd get stuck with his daughter. He refused alternate weekends. It makes me ill even to see my brother these days, knowing he abandoned his own little girl. I have tasted abandonment. You can't see it; neighbors don't know it. Even Flavia doesn't really know it.

But I do. And someday, Meg will.

The really infuriating thing about Gretchen is that she would take Derek back in a heartbeat. If the man so much as knocked on the door, Gretchen would be in there defrosting a steak, doing his laundry, and making his dentist appointments. "What's the matter with you?" I yelled at my sister-in-law once. "The man is a scum, even if he is my brother!"

"But I love him," Gretchen said miserably. Gretchen worships Derek. Her god is as inexplicable as a volcano or an earthquake. He hurts her without warning; but she still worships.

I have thought a lot lately about worship. We all have our gods: The News, Fitness, Ex-Husband. I don't know who my god is. I just don't want to be like Gretchen, and worship a dud.

Last January, my parents bought a motor home, intricately fitted as a yacht. Miniature galley, double bed that folds out over the cab, clever closets with darling drawers. (I am a sucker for cute storage. My bedroom is filled with specialized containers from mail-order catalogs.) Gloria stocked maps for the forty-eight continental states and each major city. I had had no idea how many major cities there are in America. "Are you going on a trip?" I finally asked.

"I'm going to see everything," Gloria said with a certain ferocity, as if I'd threatened to blow up the bridges on the interstates to keep her home. "From Key West to the Grand Canyon. I've stayed here and raised kids for twenty-eight years. It's enough. As soon as you're settled into a job after graduation, we're leaving." She put her hands on her hips, daring me to argue.

I try to lead my life with as little upheaval as possible. I try not to get in their way. Sometimes I think my mother is just being polite.

The plans keep expanding. Gloria is taking on America like an amoeba, spreading out over the entire continent. My father even built a special rack for all the tour guides. They're going to see everything from Eisenhower's birthplace to Elvis's bedroom.

They didn't ask me along.

* * *

When I got home, Dad was rotating between the kitchen and the living room televisions. We have TVs in every room, including the bathroom, so Dad won't risk missing any News. The curtains are pulled by day, so no stray sunshine will reflect on the screen. When I have a house of my own, I will never ever draw a drape or lower a shade.

I got out the ironing board to press my outfit for the Athletic Banquet. I had gone down to Sable Mall with Flavia and bought this adorable sky blue cotton dress, quite long, with a cut-lace white jacket. Last year at the Athletic Banquet the kids wore the uniform of their sport. This year I insisted on jacket and tie for boys, dresses for girls.

"Hi, honey." My father was frowning. He has a special frown for absorbing facts. I truly think he expects The News anchor to give him a test one day and he wants to be ready.

"Hi, Dad." I don't know why people say ironing is awful. I enjoy it. The summer gown was wrinkled and repulsive, but a few sweeps with my iron and — perfection.

Ten days of class, and grades would no longer matter. The last research paper of my life lay in my notebook, waiting to be passed in. There were more exams, but none I couldn't handle. Senior year, with Spirit and yearbook and cheerleading and everything else to handle, I took the easiest possible courses. Knowledge-retention-wise, I was in the home stretch.

31

It's probably how besieged soldiers feel when relief troops are in sight: I hear the helicopters coming, hang on! Graduate out of this war! Pass the fight to next year's class.

I went to the telephone. Of course, Jaz had just dropped me off and I had just spoken with Flavia, but there were subjects yet uncovered. "Flavia, should I wear my hair in braids or loose?"

"Braids."

"No. I'd rather wear it loose."

"Then what did you call me for?" Flavia asked. "You've always already made your decision before you ask advice."

"I called because no decision can be made without a telephone," I said.

"You're going to have some phone bill when we're all at college."

We laughed, and hung up. I put on the dress, and smoothed it. A double row of narrow braids, diagonally from my forehead to just behind my ears, would keep my hair out of my eyes, let my earrings show, and be more formal. Hair done, I came downstairs to wait for Jaz's honk.

My father looked up during an ad. "Nice dress, honey. I like that color. Going somewhere?"

I had kidded myself that he would know where I was going; that he had even saved, and perhaps even answered, the invitation to attend the Athletic Banquet. If my mother were home, she might have remembered. But Gloria is rarely home.

Dit, dit, dit, dit!

"Nobody in my graduating class will ever forget H," I told my father.

"Neither will the neighborhood," he said dryly. He turned his cheek to accept my kiss, but his eyes stayed on the reporter in Eastern Europe.

Yearbooks go to the printer months before the really good things, like Athletic Banquet, Senior Prom, or Graduation, take place. So I was doing a Senior Supplement to be mailed out in July. Jaz is a good photographer, and has his own equipment. He didn't play any sports at Westerly, so he wasn't getting any award. I assigned him to cover the banquet. He circled, knelt, and wandered the way photographers do. I admired Jaz, my table settings, my ten-foot flowery baseball player, and my friends.

Flavia came over to the cheerleaders' table to tell me how terrific everything looked, how proud I could be. "What's wrong?" I asked warily. (Flavia considers it her task to keep my ego in line; she's quite worried about what will happen to my ego when she leaves for college. "It's already half the size of Maine," she says, "without me to puncture you now and then, you're going to balloon out over the Atlantic Ocean.")

"Really," Flavia said. "Your best friend can't give you a simple compliment without you turning on her?" She folded her mouth into a pretend sneer and then she smiled and pointed.

33

My parents had come.

They had dressed up. My mother, stylish, my father, distinguished.

"Jaz went back for them," said Flavia.

Oh, Jaz! You sweetheart! I really do love you.

I waved to them. They waved back, smiling. Our usual distance.

I was not used to seeing them at school. They almost never came to a game to see me cheer. I had left my yearbook on the sofa. It was anybody's guess whether they would notice it, admire it, compliment me on it.

We clapped for field hockey, football, soccer, softball, basketball, baseball, tennis, track. Of course the world is a wimp. People's hands hurt so they stopped clapping. When Kyle got a measly little clink instead of ovations, I said to my cheerleaders, "You can train them and train them, but without a whip they just don't remember."

"The spectators," Susannah agreed, "have faded into lumps."

Everybody likes things to be done well, but they don't like to exert themselves to achieve it. I personally love exertion. I've been a cheerleader since seventh grade, and this year we lost our coach, so I was Varsity Captain *and* coach, which took a lot of time. But I loved it. I love noise, actually. The best thing about cheerleading is you get praise for making a terrible racket. Screaming is such a fine activity.

We cheerleaders jumped up, kicked our chairs

out of the way, and ignoring our long gowns, began yelling, "Kyle, Kyle, he's our man, if he can't do it, nobody can!"

Kyle was startled, to say the least, not having merited any particular attention athletically speaking. Blushing, he took his award and shuffled to his seat.

After that we had no trouble with volume levels from the audience.

We had no trouble with anything until Johnny D'Andrea accepted the baseball team award. It would go in the trophy case in the front hall, but he got to hold it for a minute.

What a changing landscape a boy is. In seventh grade Johnny was a short creep whose only skill was making disgusting noises. Now he's an Italian sculpture, dark gold skin and curly black hair.

Nobody had had the lack of sense to give a speech. Everybody else knew enough to start and stop with "Thank you." Not Johnny.

There is nothing worse than being embarrassed in public on somebody else's behalf. Johnny is good at engines, not words. We cringed. Flavia signaled "uh-oh." But Johnny, speech in hand, went to the podium and took the mike from Dr. Stefford.

"We all have great memories of high school, and most of mine are about sports. I want to thank the coach, our parents, and especially all our little brothers and sisters who have been dragged to games they don't care about, in weather they don't want to be out in."

He smiled. What a great smile! The whole audience had to reciprocate.

"Our graduating class is closing down," said Johnny softly. "Like a store after dark. Doors are shutting. People are driving away."

My class is graduating.

I had wanted our senior year to be the most memorable ever, but I had not stopped to think that that's what it would become.

Memory.

Over.

Forever.

"Good-bye," said Johnny D'Andrea to a tearful room. "And thank you."

Susannah started the cheer when I didn't: "Johnny, Johnny, he's our man, if he can't do it, no one can!" I had to clear my throat twice to get through it.

When the clapping died down, Dr. Stefford went back to the podium, carrying one of the largest bouquets I have ever seen; in school colors, purple irises, white roses, feathery ferns. I felt so sad I thought it was a funeral wreath, to lie on the coffin of our class.

"We are losing a very special person at graduation," said Dr. Stefford. "Someone with unique energy and enthusiasm. Someone who endlessly demanded *Spirit* from her classmates, and *more* Spirit, and still again — *Spirit!* Someone who wanted you to have the most wonderful senior year in the history of senior years — and pulled it off."

Jaz aimed his videocam at me.

Flavia was standing.

They were all standing.

My parents were standing.

"Miss Helen Miranda Revness," said Dr. Stefford, "from your class."

For once in my life, I did not have to lead the applause.

Four

How could a dance succeed without a girls' room?

The ballroom at Sea Storm is beautiful — crystal chandeliers and gold-wrapped mirrors — but the ladies' room has the real necessity: privacy for comparing notes, adjusting gowns, and repeating conversations. We spent at least half the prom in the ladies' room, giggling, while the boys stood around in the ballroom, waiting.

"You were so smart to have it at Sea Storm, Hallie," Susannah said. "When I think of those times we decorated the cafeteria . . ."

"Remember Junior Prom, Hallie? You got each art class to do a mural for the cafeteria walls? One was in questionable taste and Dr. Stefford made us rip it down before the dance started."

"And the year before," said Valerie, "when you made us lie down on huge paper rolls and make paper dolls of ourselves? I still have my paper doll boyfriend on my wall. 'Course we broke up the next week, but still — "

I love it when people talk about me.

All right, it's conceited. But conceit is a wonderful thing. If you don't have any, there's no bubble in you. Conceit is what you start with.

I was especially conceited about my gown, which was deep blue, almost black, tightly fitted above the waist, with a skirt in separating panels that slithered silkily when I moved. I had been shopping since January, and found it in April.

The ladies' room door opened. Marcy Hampson. I reminded myself to be friend-ish. "Marcy, I love your dress," I said, which was not true. Washed-out turquoise did not go with Marcy's complexion; it would not go with any complexion in the world.

"It's a hand-me-down," said Marcy levelly. "It doesn't fit, it's an ugly color, and you don't love it, Hallie."

Flavia said, "Oh, Marcy, that's so sad. Hallie and I have a dozen gowns between us. We would have loaned you one. You should have asked."

"You would, huh? I just bet. If I walked up to Queen Hallie in the cafeteria, you think she'd even have said Hello? Get a life." Marcy entered a stall. The flush was all too appropriate for her opinion of us.

We left en masse.

The boys were leaning against a marble pillar on

the sea side of the room. Jaz set down his drink, smiling, glad to have me back. The floor was full of dancers. He cut through.

In seventh grade we read *Romeo and Juliet*. The play just irritated the rest of the class. They all thought Juliet should have been more sensible. Everybody complained during the exam. "Can we just write 'bunch of crap'?" they demanded. It was no bunch of crap to me.

I held out my hands and Jaz walked faster. "Love," I said to Flavia, "involves a mathematical equation. A geometric progression. When you love a boy, and he loves you, all love multiplies. Friend, parent, classmate love: You swim in love, like high tide."

"Hallie, that's so sweet! Write that in Jaz's yearbook. Speaking of love, I have to tell you something. I broke up with Michael during dinner."

"You what?"

"We've been meaning to break up for weeks. We don't want to be tied down at college."

"The night of the prom?"

"We were afraid if we were still going together for the prom, we'd go together all summer. I have to start my college career unattached, Hallie." (Flavia never refers to it as merely "college." It's her college "career.") "Michael wanted to wait till the end of summer," she explained. "But that would be too wrenching. We need adjustment time prior to college orientation."

"If anybody tried to break up with me the night of the prom," I told Flavia, "I'd have said to Fluff off. I can't believe you didn't discuss this with me. What were all those hundreds of phone calls for?"

"I did tell you, you just didn't listen. All you think about is senior year. The rest of us are past that. Michael and I are still friends. It was very mutual."

"But you'll be alone enough as it is. New state, new life, new dorm, new people. I can't understand dumping a boyfriend. What if you can't get back to being a couple? What if you're all alone forever?"

Flavia looked confused. "But I don't want to be a couple."

I needed time to think about that one. But of course everybody followed Jaz over, because I travel in a crowd, and how were they to know that for once I didn't want crowdship?

The band was very loud. I want them loud when I'm dancing, but not when I'm talking. It irks me that the band does not read my mind and adjust accordingly.

Sea Storm has a glass wall facing a frothing Atlantic Ocean. Salt spray turns the glass opaque every high tide. "I spent all last summer washing that," said Michael. "This summer, though, I'm parking. At last, I get to drive a Jaguar myself, Jaz. Tell all your rich friends to give me big tips."

Jaz smiled and changed the subject. "Anyone else have a summer job?"

Everybody likes the summer job topic. Especially my parents. *What job interviews are you scheduling? You have to have a job before we leave on our trip. Are you interested in working at a restau-*

rant? Factory? Retail store? Do you want us to help?
No, I just want to lie out with Flavia and get a tan.

"When are your parents leaving, Hallie?" Susannah asked.

"Probably not till September or October. I'm supposed to stay with my brother. But what I'm going to do is throw parties. One for every night I'm on my own."

"I wish I were going to be around," Susannah cried. "But of course I'll be in California." She beamed. "Going to fraternity parties."

"Do they have fraternities in California?" asked Flavia. "That sounds awfully East Coast. I bet you'll do something we never even heard of."

"I bet you're right," Susannah said, with gestures that proved even hands should sometimes go on swear diets.

"Who'll you invite to your bashes, Hallie?" Flavia teased. "We'll be at college. You'll have to have a whole new set of friends." Flavia kissed Michael's cheek in a sisterly way. How soft she looked, with her pale gold hair and ivory complexion. During the divorce, despair turned Gretchen into a stringy-haired, swollen-eyed hag. Here was Flavia, her romance over and not so much as an un-mascara-ed eyelash. As for Michael, he was quiet but did not seem upset. My brothers would have been throwing bottles at this stage. Jaz was unsurprised; clearly Michael had told him. In his annoying boy's way, Jaz said nothing to me. Saying nothing on a vital topic is just like a boy. If silence is golden, boys are rich.

"Now," Susannah said, linking one arm through Michael's and one through Flavia's. "I want to hear about this split. We need details. The night of the prom? You two would have been in the running for Class Couple if Jaz here hadn't moved to town."

Flavia spread her hands, preface to an intellectual explanation. "I want college to be open. All things possible."

"You mean you want to date other boys," Susannah clarified.

"College," Flavia said, "is a thousand things we haven't seen or tried yet. Michael and I don't want to be fastened to somebody in another state who'd dictate our answers or our feelings." Flavia gripped her own wrists as if they were tennis rackets. "I feel almost sick with nerves and yet I'm so excited!" The soft gold aura vanished; even her bones seemed to re-align. Flavia looked older, as if she had already graduated and moved on. "I'm so hot and eager. I feel as if I'm going out to commit crimes instead of going to college. I don't want anything from home holding me back."

The rest laughed breathlessly. It was *exactly* how they felt, they said eagerly; it was *perfect*!

They had great lives. How dare they talk of disposing of their lives, like paper cups? My hair, beneath the firm attachment of its narrow braiding, quivered aginst the scalp. My hands dampened. My mother . . . was Gloria disposing of this life, too?

"Hallie," Susannah said, "aren't you afraid you're missing something by not going to college?"

"Let's don't have this conversation again."

"Hallie, I worry about you. What's going to happen to you? What are you going to do with your life? There's nothing here. What can you do in this town but waitress, clerk, bookkeep, and clean? You're meant for better things."

Flavia took it up. "Hallie, if you stay here, a local forever — "

"You're a local, too! We're all locals but Jaz."

"But not forever," said Susannah. "We're getting out."

"It's not a coffin. Nobody's nailing me into a suffocating little life where I'll rot."

"Nobody thinks you'll rot," said Jaz soothingly. He fingerpainted on my arm. "It's just that you have possibilities, Hallie. You — "

"Possibilities!" I jerked away, hair swirling like black snow. "How generous of you, Jaz. Are you quoting your mother, perhaps? *If you got that little girl out of this town . . . If you fixed her up and educated her . . .*"

"Hallie, stop it. Nobody said that. Nobody ever will." He moved me almost roughly back from the others, behind marble pillars, into the shadows. "I love you, Helen Miranda," breathed Jaz, using both names like a dare. We touched with exploring fingers, and our lips pressed as if forever.

Drums, keyboard, and guitars reached a screaming peak. We held each other against the assault of noise, deafened — and it stopped. We gasped for breath, as if all that volume had sucked our lungs dry.

"Ladies and gentlemen," shouted the bandleader, voice shuddering through the speakers, "the votes are in. You have elected, for your Prom King and Queen . . ."

The drumroll seemed too short for the occasion. In fact, the whole last month of senior year seemed too short for the occasion.

". . . Hallie Revness and Jasper Innes."

"We did it, Helen Miranda," Jaz whispered. "It's our year. All the way." His hand caressed my bare back, fingers lodged just below the opening of the dress, sending little shocks up my spine. We walked out into the spotlight. I went slowly, to make it last, but our friends pushed us forward, rushing it along. We were King and Queen almost before I had a chance to taste it.

I should have kept a journal, I thought dizzily. Written down every sweet thing Jaz said. Kept a calendar of football games in November, skiing in January. How well he was named. Jasper. Precious stone.

"Look out!" Flavia shrieked.

Glitter confetti pelted us from all sides. That was one thing I had not organized. Jaz tried to shield himself with his hands. "Not me!" he yelled. Nobody listened. Both of us were drenched. My reflection in the dark glass wall sparkled like a thousand prisms.

Jaz adjusted my crown, weaving black hair through the golden filigree. "Diamonds in your hair, Hallie," he said, kissing me in front of a hundred witnesses.

Immediately all the girls claimed a need to freshen up. The ladies' room was packed to the walls of the stalls.

Nobody freshened. Everybody gathered around to discuss the meaning of the word diamond in that particular context; whether Jaz knew (taking into account the supreme slowness of boys) that diamonds mean rings and weddings. Everybody discussed where the romance was actually going. (That was a big word senior year: *going*. "But is it *going* anywhere?" we liked to say.)

It's going somewhere, I thought, my heart rushing to a misty future of wedding gowns, first apartments, and Jaz.

The girls stepped back for me when I left the ladies' room.

That's Hallie.

Queen of the Prom.

Isn't she beautiful?

Aren't she and Jaz gorgeous together?

46

Five

Jaz, bored with rehearsal, ran up and down the wall, a favorite occupation of boys. Westerly is laced with shoe prints; boys like to point out their best treads. Royce and Derek used to come by for old times' sake and admire *their* prints. "Come on, Hallie!" Jaz yelled. "Head of the line for us."

"Small towns," the coach said wearily, "go by height. Get to the back of the line where you belong, Jasper." Coach is one of those teachers who would always rather be doing something else, preferably with somebody else. We don't use his name; he is his sport.

"If we go by height, I'm not with Helen Miranda. I'll squat. I'll cut my feet off at the ankles."

Coach is not amused by time wasting. He dressed Jaz down with every word on my diet. If the principal had been around, the coach would have been in trouble, but principals are like police; never there when you need one. "In high school you're tallest,

47

so get your body back there." The boys passed Jaz like a football, pummeling his ribs. Coach approved.

Each girl was counting heads to see who her boy partner would be, ready to fudge on heights if she got stuck with a drip.

Susannah ended up with Lennox, who is destined for drugs or jail, having had plenty of each already. "I'll be wearing high heels!" called Susannah desperately. "I'll be two inches taller. I have to move back."

Everybody shifted, not wanting Lennox. I looked to see who Jaz got and whether to be jealous. But we have more boys than girls, so Jaz's partner was Gordon. Jaz signaled me, extended arms spelling letters.

Susannah said, "I can't make out the words, Hallie, but the content is clear. The guy is nuts about you."

Flavia waved a white paper. "I got a letter from my roommate-to-be, Hallie! She's from Las Vegas. I cannot picture school in Las Vegas. Do you suppose they have things like Brownie Scouts and — "

"Flavia!" yelled Coach. "You're valedictorian! Get up here at the head of the line where you belong."

"If I'm not first," Flavia agreed, "the hell with it."

Marcy Hampson came running down the hall, late. Everybody was satisfied with his or her partner; nobody wanted to let Marcy in. She shuffled around, trying to break in like a car onto the turnpike at rush hour.

High school for me is gold; for Marcy, it's just a scuff on the wall. The least I could do was be friendish. "Here, Marcy, get in front of me," I said, giving up Kyle. Marcy accepted with hatred instead of gratitude. I stepped back and got a new partner.

Johnny D'Andrea.

My heart sank. He'd be rude and spoil graduation.

But no. As if we were grown-ups — only by accident in a high school hallway — Johnny gave me a chaste and neighborly hug.

"Oh, Johnny!" Tears filled my eyes.

"I know. I feel misty myself. I can't believe it's over."

A big hairy brown gorilla entered the lobby. "Pizza delivery for Jaz Innes?" said the gorilla, holding an armload of cardboard boxes.

"Jaz!" Coach said. "What is this?"

"Pepperoni with extra cheese. I ordered twenty." Jaz galloped toward the gorilla. Passing me, he said sternly, "No kissing other guys, Helen Miranda."

"I don't like pepperoni," complained Coach. "Why didn't you order sausage and onions?"

"Hey, would I forget?" said the gorilla, peeling off his mask. It was Wayne Morgan, a football star from two years ago. He handed Coach his own (presumably sausage and onion) pizza. "Hey, Wayne, awww-right!" shouted boys who'd been on teams with him.

Wayne, for whom I cheered in soccer, football, and basketball. I must have screamed *Wayne,*

Wayne, he's our man, if he can't do it, nobody can! a million times. And meant it, every time. What a crush I had once on Wayne! I thought he would go into sports, be a commentator, play in the majors. Wayne, two years after graduation, dressed as a gorilla, delivering pizza.

Dr. Stefford came to see how graduation rehearsal was progressing (it wasn't) and to get his share of pizza.

Flavia waved her pizza wedge. "Dr. Stefford, when we go on stage to get our diplomas, and you read off our extracurricular activities, awards, and honors — "

"Nobody cares, Flavia," muttered Johnny.

" — will you also be announcing what college each of us is going to?"

Johnny wiped his hands on his jeans as if wiping away Flavia.

"Not everybody," said Dr. Stefford, "made the choice to go to college, Flavia, and I'm not comfortable — "

"It should be announced," said Flavia. "We represent the success of this school system."

"What are the rest of us?" demanded Johnny. "Failures of the school system? You just want the world to know you're going to Princeton. You'd especially like the world to know you turned down Dartmouth and Cornell, huh, Flavia?"

Flavia stepped out of line for an unobstructed view of Johnny. "You're just jealous because you're never going to do anything in your little local life but change the spark plugs in somebody else's motor, Johnny D'Andrea."

Johnny, like Derek, responded with his fists.

"Don't, Johnny," said Marcy quickly, catching his arm with long, slim fingers. "Flavia isn't worth it."

Dr. Stefford glared at Flavia, a new experience for them both. But it was Johnny he ordered to apologize. Proof, if we still needed it, that college kids count; the rest of us are just spark plug changers.

For a moment I thought there would be no graduation rehearsal. The kids aligned with Johnny would throw their pizzas at the wall and storm out. Marcy's beautiful hand lay quietly on Johnny's arm. It did not seem a match for the rest of her. Johnny took a deep breath. "I'm sorry, Flavia," he said neutrally. We were amazed. Flavia flushed and muttered, "My fault, Johnny." Then we were *really* amazed.

Coach began clapping a march rhythm. "Let's get this show on the road. Down the center aisle, two by two, keep an even distance between couples, seven pairs to a riser, class officers to the right."

Flavia marched first, alone, as seriously as an explorer looking for the Northwest Passage. Chin high, shoulders back.

Wayne, in his gorilla suit, marched in place, stomping loudly. He whacked his chest with his gorilla head for added percussion.

"This is so bizarre," Marcy said. "I can't believe I am actually graduating from such a weird school. Forty-six kids holding pizza wedges, a gorilla keep-

51

ing time, and Flavia taking on the world."

Johnny smiled and shook his head, obviously agreeing with her.

Wayne beamed at me. "Hey, Hallie! Babe! How are ya?"

"Good, thanks, Wayne. How are you?"

"I miss high school, Hallie. We used to have such fun. It's a blast being back. Where are you going to college next fall?"

"I'm not going, Wayne." What a relief when Johnny and I had to start down the aisle; his gorilla suit frightened me. I couldn't think why. I used to love Halloween costumes; this was no different.

Halfway down the aisle, Johnny said, "Why aren't you going, Hallie?"

"This is enough school for me. I don't want more assignments, classes, teachers, or labs."

"Me, either. I've wanted to quit since I turned sixteen. My father said he wouldn't give me a job at the marina and he'd see nobody else in the state gave me one, if I quit without my diploma."

I could imagine Mr. D'Andrea saying that. "Do it my way or get out." But from love. Wanting the best for his son. If only my parents would say things like that to me. But my parents feel they're teaching by example, whatever that means.

The best.

How many times had the school, the team, and I expected "the best" from Wayne Morgan, and gotten it?

What "best" had Wayne expected from life?

Flavia was laughing at me and pointing. "Silly Hallie," she said from the podium. "Weeping because high school is over."

But I was not weeping for high school. I was weeping for Wayne.

The real graduation robe was heavy as sail canvas. I needed Johnny's arm. Royce and Derek slid out of their seats and squatted in the aisles, shouldering videocams. Dad aimed his Polaroid. My mother smiled.

"Remember when we were little and the neighborhood used to play hide-and-seek, Hallie?" Johnny said suddenly. "How you always hid behind the forsythia bushes?" Memories of childhood, dim and dusty and summery, surfaced. Would high school one day be that distant? But what would happen in between?

Those late summer evenings when the cry would shrill from somebody's porch. Not American: "Hey, you guys, come on in!" Ancient words, like a sacred inheritance. "All-y, all-y, in come free," I repeated.

"Wasn't free," said Johnny. "High school cost me serious pain."

We moved slowly and with dignity, like a wedding march.

"I wish Orrin were here," I said to Johnny.

"Since when have you cared about Orrin?" Johnny nodded to his grandparents, uncles, aunts, and an entire row of cousins, every one of whom took a photograph of us. "Immortalized with a D'Andrea," said Johnny cheerfully. "And you thought it was good with Jaz."

We sat on folding chairs on the risers. Jaz, directly behind me, pressed his kneecaps into my spine and tapped a bony Morse code. *Dit, dit, dit, dit,* he spelled; *dit dah.*

One by one, we rose for our diplomas. I stared at each fellow graduate as if I had never seen the person before. "Relax," murmured Johnny. "We're almost done. Another few minutes and we're gone."

"That's the trouble. Another few minutes and I'm gone."

"Helen Miranda Revness," announced the Superintendent of Schools. Enough flashbulbs went off to illuminate stadiums. The mortarboard was difficult to balance. I walked slowly each direction. Graduation was nothing but a handshake. The diploma was not rolled parchment, but a black leather book with no pages. *No more classes, no more books, no more teachers' dirty looks.* What had been partly true each June, was forever true today.

Like Flavia, Jaz received a Presidential academic medal, a State Achievement medal on a scarlet and gold ribbon, an Honors pin, and a Mathematics Scholar parchment. I applauded till my palms hurt. "I haven't clapped this much since you won the States," I whispered to Johnny.

He nodded. "I'll never forget that last inning. The

most exciting ten minutes of my life."

Flavia muttered, "Probably the *last* exciting ten minutes of your life, too."

Flavia, don't, I thought. Why say things like that? What's the point?

"I could knock you off the stage, Flavia," Johnny said, "and ruin your graduation speech, but because I'm nice, unlike you, I'll pass."

I closed my mind. I hate unpleasant things, especially when somebody I like is responsible.

Flavia had worked on her valedictory speech for weeks, keeping it secret, insisting it was brilliant. Nobody doubted that. I could not wait to hear my best friend's analysis of the year I had organized. But Flavia did not mention me. She did not even mention senior year. The only value she placed on high school was as passage to college. And the only thing she talked about — to a class from which barely half were going on — was college.

Gloria is nothing if not an organizer. She put on a barbecue for fifty-four relatives, old friends, and neighbors. Everyone with a gift for me. Life should always have that agenda.

Royce and his wife Jen, who graduated from Westerly High ten years ago, had dressed little Leighton and Emmett in tiny white graduation suits. Leighton and Emmett (not family names — they're supposed to sound distinguished; Royce of mailbox-smashing fame plans for his sons to be lawyers and senators) are the center of their lives. Jen quit work when Leighton and Emmett were born, and now speaks disparagingly of "summer mothers," who arrive in town for two weeks of "quality time" on the beach, trying to make up for the "neglect" of the previous year.

Leighton was obsessed by the barbecue coals, which he wanted to hold, and Emmett decided the time had come for a confrontation with the cat. Since coals burn and the cat bites, it was a sad afternoon for Leighton and Emmett.

Derek didn't have baby Meg, but some bimbo named Kerry. Kerry had a definite look of one in need of drugs. How I missed Gretchen. I wanted a family undivided. I felt a sudden need to tell Derek this. Derek, who is not subtle, told me where to go. Immediately fifty-four people were either pro-Derek (Gretchen wasn't good enough for you, dear), or pro-Gretchen (if you'd died, Derek, at least she'd have the life insurance).

My mother, scooping Leighton away from the barbecue yet again, said, "And you wonder why I need a few months on the other side of the Rocky Mountains."

We laughed.

It's so rare for us to share anything. I touched her arm and did not feel, as usual, that I was trespassing on private territory. My father even said, "You were beautiful, honey. I was proud of you."

"Really, Daddy?"

"Look at these photographs!" He studied the sheaf of Polaroids he had taken, arranging and rearranging his pictures.

I stood breathing, live, beside him. He preferred the copies. In an unexpected leap of the heart, I felt sorry for my father instead of for myself.

It was the best he could do.

Six

Summer hurtled past.

It was no summer of childhood, days long and sunny, full of slow naps and yawning afternoons.

The days leaped forward: They seemed to have no space inside them. I arrived at the beach, put on sun block, and it was time to go. Got in the Jaguar with Jaz, and we were home. Finished supper and it was midnight.

"Why are you so frantic?" Jaz said to me.

"What are you talking about?"

"This was supposed to be a leisurely summer, Hallie. Instead, you yank me from one thing to another."

"If it were up to you, we'd just lie on the sand and talk about college!" I had been dumb enough to think college talk would end with the school year. No. College talk quadrupled.

Flavia talked endlessly about Kris of Las Vegas. "My roommate," she'd say contentedly. Kris had written three letters which Flavia kept in her beach bag, for ready reference. Flavia would show the letters to anybody who asked, and maddeningly enough, everybody asked. Kris wrote in some irritation to say that Las Vegas was a wonderful place to grow up, and Yes, they had Brownie Scouts, and No, they didn't gamble at their meetings, they went on desert hikes and studied Indian civilization, so there.

Jaz had no dorm assignment. He had a letter telling him eventually he would get one. There was space on campus for Jasper Innes; he was not to panic.

Jaz panicked. "What if I'm stuck in a motel," he would say anxiously, "or rooming in some old lady's house? Dorm life is what I'm looking forward to most."

Jaz and I gave a party at his private beach for the whole class. The surprise treat was a movie, on which I had labored for weeks, retaped from a hundred old films that mothers had been taking of our class since kindergarten. Us: from age five to age eighteen. I loved every frame.

Our class, I thought, will be like the Pledge of Allegiance. One nation, under God, indivisible.

The Innes house is very modern, very high, very striking. It also blocks the ocean view for a dozen families. When the house went up, the whole town hoped for a really decent hurricane to sweep the Innes family out to sea, where they belonged. It seemed a century ago that I had watched the construction and hoped for that myself.

"Remember when your plumbing froze, Jaz?" teased Flavia. "And you had six unusable luxury bathrooms?"

He laughed. "I found out there's nothing more entertaining than The Fall of the Ignorant Summer Person."

Johnny D'Andrea brought Amy, Candy, Matt, Rob, and Billy in his truck. The truck is small; they were really packed in.

"Hello, John," said Mr. Innes, shaking hands. (I never think of Johnny as John; it turns him into a whole other person.) "Nobody drives cars any more," Mr. Innes observed. "Just tiny trucks with tires big enough for invasions of Europe."

Johnny laughed. "I only invade the woods. I drive offroad. Places like Mott Hill or along the utility lines. Way in the woods."

Mrs. Innes shuddered. "But what if your truck breaks down? You could drive off some ledge, break an axle, and nobody could get a tow in!"

Johnny laughed, nodding. "Neighbors would carry in food for awhile, but they'd get tired of it, and you'd just die up there. Place is strewn with rusting cars where nature won." Johnny had changed generations. An adult D'Andrea, entertaining adult Inneses.

Most of the class stayed half the night, but Johnny left after only an hour. The marina was too busy to abandon for anything so frivolous as a party. He stuck his hand out to Jaz. "Good luck in college if I don't see you again, Jaz." Johnny jogged lightly out of the house and drove away.

"I always said the size of the tires is inversely proportional to the size of the brain, but perhaps I was wrong," said Mr. Innes. "That boy doesn't seem dysfunctional."

Jaz closed his eyes. "Thank God you didn't say that in front of him, Dad."

"So sad," said Mrs. Innes. "He's still a child. Only hours out of high school. And too busy to play."

"He doesn't want to play," Jaz objected. "School was just an annoyance for Johnny."

Mrs. Innes shuddered. "Imagine not loving school! What kind of life do you have, if you don't go to college?"

My parents yelled at me for not having job interviews. They'd leave the newspaper classifieds open on the breakfast table with employment opportunities circled in red Magic Marker.

"I never interfere in your lives!" I yelled back. "How come all of a sudden you're interfering in mine?"

"Because we'll be away for weeks! Because you are a high school graduate, Helen Miranda! Because you have to have a job."

Food Bag needed another grocery checker.

I did walk inside. Laurie Copp was at the cash register. Laurie, my graduating class Laurie, on the cheerleading squad with me for two years, wearing a brown uniform that did not fit. Gunk smeared on the pocket, her hands black with newspaper ink from the heavy Sunday papers she had sorted and piled. People argued about change, whined because she was out of their brand of cigarette, and chewed gum in her face.

"Hey, Hallie. Do something for ya?" She gave me a big grin and rang up the charges for a man buying girlie magazines and sugar-free gum.

I bought a quart of milk. "You like working here?" I asked.

She shrugged. "It's work. I'm saving for a car. They've offered me a manager's position if I stay six months."

A grimy oil-stained man thrust a ten-dollar bill in her hand. "Unleaded on four," he said. She rang it up, opening the gas pump for him. His grimy hand had touched hers. She didn't appear to notice, didn't rush to the bathroom to scrub it off. Six months? I thought. I couldn't do this six minutes.

"Food Bag isn't hiring," I told my mother.

Flavia and I staked a claim on the best part of the beach, and whichever kids were not at work spread their towels next to us. We had seaweed fights and towel-shaking wars. The concession did a great business in french fries which we fed to sea gulls so they would swoop in and out like sky choreography.

One Sunday when the radio played the top forty of the year, I telephoned every single kid in the class.

"We have to remember the Songs of Our Last Summer," I coaxed. Even Marcy Hampson showed up, and Johnny D'Andrea actually took an hour from work. There was a total of nine box radios out on the sand — even one is forbidden; you're supposed to use Walkmans and not bother your neighbors with your noise. But the lifeguard had graduated with Wayne the gorilla and sang right along, so the summer mothers had nobody to complain to. Little kids danced on the sand while we danced in the waves.

July whipped past.

We said good-bye to Valerie, who left in the morning. Toasted Gordon, who left the following afternoon. Found out Candy and Max were already gone, and hadn't bothered to say good-bye.

My mother, whom I had hardly seen all senior year, was now home constantly. "I was home this much before," she insisted. "You were the one who was never here." Sitting on her exercise bike, she'd pedal furiously to nowhere, staring at a blank wall. (Interior decorating bores Gloria. If she ever went inside the Innes house, with its wire sculptures and modern art, she'd fall over laughing.) "Find a job."

"Mother, it's barely August."

"Your friends will be gone in two weeks."

Summer ending as fast as senior year. How could that be?

"I want you settled in a job, Helen Miranda. Royce and Jen are ready for you to move over there. You'll have a choice of cars: Daddy's or mine."

"I don't need a job yet. I'll wait till everybody's gone."

"Your father and I want to plan our departure date, and we can't until you're settled. Do not go to the beach tomorrow. Interview. Sea Storm is looking for waitresses."

I imagined myself waiting on next year's seniors. "May I help you, please?" "I'm sorry, we don't have pizza." "Would you like anything else?" Picking up the ten cents habitually left as a non-tip.

The group on the beach dwindled. Towels were stationed closer together. People who weren't going to college had gotten jobs, or entered the Army, or simply disappeared. A class of forty-seven became thirty-five, became twenty, became ten.

For months every strategy was aimed toward being alone with Jaz; to have no destination but each other. Now whenever I was alone with Jaz, I got weepy. I knew he had to go to college; I had always known it. But I lost my grip. All he had to do was mention college in any context (packing, phone number, classes) and I'd scream, "Shut up about college, Jaz!" Or else I'd wrap my arms around him, bury my face in his shoulder, and sob, "Don't go!"

"Listen," Jaz said one day, "forget the public beach. You and I have to talk. Come to my beach. We'll be alone."

An empty beach frightens me: primeval, like the

beginning of time. Or the end. "It's no fun at a private beach. You need a crowd for a beach. Kids throwing sand, lifeguards blowing whistles, everybody dropping down beside us and sharing their Pepsi."

I refused to go to his house. His mother would be gloating, her eyes saying, Hah! Thought you had him! I put him in a college a thousand miles away, so there!

Once I whispered to Jaz, "I can't do it."

"Can't do what?"

"I don't know, Jaz. Whatever's out there."

"Hallie, you've organized an entire school for an entire year. You can do anything."

Jaz stayed away from the subject of college. Every now and then I would find him avoiding me, seeking out people like Michael, Flavia, or Susannah. He could talk to them about college, and they would be just as excited, and full of dreams.

Flavia said, "You realize you're doing the hard way what Michael and I did the easy way."

"What are you talking about?" I said irritably.

"You're breaking up with Jaz. You know you can't be tied down when he's a thousand miles away. So you're ending it. But you shouldn't do it like this, Hallie. You're going to be bitter and angry and he'll — "

"I am not breaking up with Jaz! He is my life! Shut up about it, Flavia."

Flavia said mildly, "For somebody on a swear diet, you sure have a lot of cursing you'd like to do."

"Fluff off!"

We laughed.

But not really.

If everybody loves swearing, everybody loves shopping more.

We stood in the center of Sable Mall and admired the store displays. From The Gap, Flavia bought a sweater that looked right for college. At Lumberjack, Flavia bought a State of Maine pine tree mug for Kris. At the Record Shoppe, we decided regretfully we could afford no more CDs.

"I forgot to ask at my college interview," Flavia said, "whether there are good shopping malls in Princeton. Actually, I didn't forget; I thought it might make the wrong impression. I asked how large the library was instead." We giggled. I thought, it won't change; she'll go to Princeton, but we'll still always be able to shop together. Our thoughts matched.

"Oh, Hallie," Flavia said, "I'm going to miss you so much. All summer I've been on the verge of crying. I keep fending it off, like the enemy. This summer feels so quivery!"

If we had not had our arms full of Flavia's shopping, we would have embraced. It would have been an embrace as intimate as any with Jaz. Friendship close as love.

"What will it be like for you when I'm at college? When everybody's gone? Hallie, you brush it off, but we'll be off having a blast and getting educated and you'll sit here."

She had ruined it.

"What will you do?" Flavia went on, relentless and unobservant as a parent.

"Why do I have to *do* something?"

"Because there are twenty-four hours in each day, and your brain will dry up if you don't use it."

The mall made its mall racket around us: shoes clicking, cash register drawers closing, Muzak humming, babies wailing. "My brain isn't going to change, Flavia."

"*My* brain had better change. I have to keep up with Kris now instead of you."

I hated her. "Go to your damn college and see if I care," I said, feeling like a skeleton. All bones. No flesh, no skin to protect me. I hated her even more for making me break the swear diet.

"If you stay in the village, you'll be one hundred percent local, Hallie. It's the kiss of death. You'll marry some forklift operator and earn money selling door-to-door cosmetics. You'll play bingo. Sunday afternoons you'll drive to the marina in your new truck and admire other people's yachts. You'll look back at high school as the best years of your life."

Flavia's teeth were perfect from years of orthodontia. Perhaps I should rearrange Flavia's face. (That was Royce's line when he started a fight on the soccer field: "I rearranged *his* jaw!") How satisfying it would be.

"And they *will* have been the best years," said Flavia urgently. "You're finished if you don't go to college. You're my friend and I want the best for you."

"The best! You're trying to stomp on me."

"I am not. You're trying to stomp on me! You want me to fail. You want me to be homesick. You want Kris to laugh at me, and you want my clothes to be wrong, and my parents to run out of money. You want me to have to come back, and stay here like *you*."

I stomped out of Sable Mall.

Flavia staggered after me, loaded down like a bag lady. "Somebody whose best years are already finished," she yelled. "Well, you're wrong, Helen Miranda! I'm going to *be* somebody."

"I'd rather stay with Gretchen than Royce and Jen," I told my mother.

"Why? Because Gretchen is so busy and so distracted she won't notice what you're up to? I think not. Now go find a job, Helen Miranda."

I began to hate the name Helen Miranda. Hallie was a girl who had fun on the beach; Helen Miranda was a drudge, an employee. I didn't know her. I didn't want to know her.

"I hope that Flavia going to Princeton means we've heard the last of her opinions," my mother said one day, pedaling madly toward the blank wall. "I am sick of her telling you that without college your life is pitiful and your future is empty." (Flavia particularly thinks stationary bikes — symbols of a life going nowhere — are pitiful.) "Where did you look for a job today, Helen Miranda?"

"I was too busy today having a fight with Flavia."

"I can readily imagine that."

I don't often tell my mother anything, but I found myself admitting, "There are whole days when the nicest I feel toward Flavia is friend-ish."

My mother pedaled harder. "Summer before college is hard on everybody. They're scared and you're envious. We'd still send you, you know. Do you want to reconsider? Your father heard on the news the other day that the state branches have openings."

"No, I don't want to reconsider! And I'm not envious."

Flavia's right about one thing, I thought. Senior year I had no swearing to do because senior year was flawless. Here in my supposed-to-be-perfect summer, the inside of me is one solid swear!

Relax. Calm down. It's just Life. No big deal.

"If you don't want a job," my mother said, "you could be Meg's baby-sitter. It would save Gretchen a lot of money, and Meg would grow up in our family after all."

I shuddered to think what Flavia would say if I ended up a baby-sitter while she was getting her master's degree.

Seven

The remaining days of summer collapsed into hours. I tried to savor them, extend them, but each was a final.

Final day sailing.

Final tennis game.

Final movie and popcorn.

I helped Jaz pack. Filled out an address book for him, in case he actually did write letters. I baked him three dozen chocolate-chip cookies to take. He and Michael polished them off that afternoon.

The last afternoon.

Before he left.

Before Flavia left.

Before they all left.

"I have presents for you," Jaz said, so pleased with his gifts he kept his eyes on the package instead of me. "Open this one first." He handed me a gift hidden in his beach towel — square like a book.

My heart fell.

Don't be a book! I thought. Oh, Jaz, I want something glittering and sacred. A ring that says *love forever*. A silver frame with our initials entwined below our Prom King and Queen photograph.

Sea gulls screamed and outboard motors gunned.

I slid the ribbons off the corner and peeled back the wrapping.

Writing paper?

I wanted an immortal token of love, and he'd bought writing paper? I'd never had a reason to write a letter. I used the phone so much that Royce and Derek used to say I should compile my phone calls the way in olden days people printed their diaries. *The Collected Phone Calls of Hallie Revness*; definitely a best-seller.

I wanted to rip the paper in half. Instead I said brightly, "Think you'll write back, Jasper Innes?"

"Don't call me by my full name. You sound like my mother. As if I forgot to take out the trash. Whenever I get a letter from you, I'll write back one of equal length and interest. Deal?"

We kissed to seal the deal.

"Now open the other one."

If he's gone and bought me a fountain pen, I thought, opening the second present, I will kick the swear diet forever.

No. It was a jade necklace. Green as underwater. The color of the ocean: cold and dangerous. I gathered my hair into a ponytail while Jaz put the jade around my neck, carefully fixing the tiny catch. Then he fluffed out my hair over my shoulders again.

"It's lovely, Jaz. I'll wear it forever." I had only thin, light necklaces: silver or gold chains, perhaps with a pendant. The jade weighed like a collar.

"My mother helped me pick it out," Jaz said happily.

Just what I didn't want to know.

Perhaps the sea-green jade was appropriate after all; I felt as if I were drowning.

"I'll miss you," Jaz said huskily, and he buried his face in my hair.

Only five of us were still around.

"Aren't we having a Very Last Party?" Flavia cried. "Hallie, I can't believe you didn't plan a Very Last, just for us!"

Why aren't you throwing a party for me? I thought. Why don't *I* get the farewell party? Why should I always be the one to organize? "County fair's on," I said. "We can go to the fireworks instead."

Oh, what a great idea! they said. Fried dough and merry-go-rounds. Ferris wheels and Swinging Death. What a fine farewell it would be.

So we went: Jaz and me, Flavia, Susannah, and Michael.

We ate till we could eat no more, and went on rides till we were dizzy and staggering. (Both good excuses for hanging even tighter to your boyfriend.)

After dark came fireworks.

We spread blankets over the hood of Susannah's father's car because it was widest. Lying with our backs against the windshield, we watched the tapestry in the sky. Silver showers. Golden stars.

"Beauty," I whispered to Jaz, "that instantly passes. Like a monarch butterfly crossing the garden."

"Like this summer," Jaz agreed. "Like childhood. We thought it lasted so long, and it's over."

"Oooooooh, philosophy," Flavia cried. "Deep profound thoughts. Good preparation, though. Who else is taking Philosophy 101 first semester?"

Everybody, including Jaz, abandoned fireworks to discuss college.

I could not stand it. "I'm going to look around," I told them. Nobody paid any attention. Even Jaz hardly noticed when I slid off the hood and disappeared into the dark. I wandered between two taco stands and kiddie-kart rides. A carnie, backlit by the Ferris wheel, was green and squat like a toad. His teeth were half rotted, and his ridged fingernails curled like weapons.

They'll go to college. They'll leave me here with people like this.

I bought three neon-lit, plastic-tube necklaces, draping them in my hair. The colors slid around inside the tubes like mercury in a thermometer.

I went back. "The only stumbling block is what to major in," Jaz was saying. "I have to be properly prepared."

I climbed onto the car hood and stood over his

face. "Love your halos," said Jaz, grabbing my ankle and chewing on it.

"Please," Michael said, "keep the displays in the sky."

"You're just jealous," Jaz said.

"You're right," Michael said, eyes on Flavia. I had never heard him utter a single syllable of loss about Flavia. I don't think Flavia had either; she seemed truly startled. Merry-go-round music mixed with crying babies. Ice-cream bells rang between the booms of the fireworks. "Just don't think about me," she said, patting him like a spaniel.

What a sentence. If Jaz thought about anyone other than me, I would put a knife through him.

"I have plans," Flavia said. "I'm going places. I can't be tied down. I'm starting a new life with new people."

Why couldn't my friends be happy with the *old* life and the *old* people? All my jealousy of the shopping, the dorm, the roommate from Las Vegas, emerged. "You're not the only one Flavia's giving up, Michael," I said. "Flavia's giving me up, too. She wants new best friends in this great new life."

"I am not giving you up!" Flavia cried. "Can't I have two lives? Can't I add friends? Why do you have to be so possessive? Haven't you heard of spreading your wings?"

The carnival's shimmering beauty turned into discarded napkins in the tall grass, a stink of grease and beer, taut faces of transient hawkers.

I tasted the truth like fried dough and candy apples. If I did not possess Jaz and Flavia, *who was there?*

Jaz took me straight home. "Do you mind if I don't come in?" he said. "I'm really tired."

Not come in.

I do not think I have ever minded anything so much. He would not be home till Thanksgiving. Ninety-nine days. I had marked them on my wall calendar. I wanted to hold him and be held, to weep, and comfort his weeping.

And he did not want to come in. Jaz had done no counting toward Thanksgiving. His countdown was over.

How difficult life would be if you could not lie easily. How do people manage, who cannot fib? "I don't mind," I said. I lifted my face for a kiss.

"Come to the house at eight. We'll be packed and ready."

"Eight," I repeated.

He ran back to the Jag, eyes and feet on his departure to college.

All that stuff about love being songs and bells ringing is wrong. Love is helplessness. You're there, he isn't. You stay, he leaves.

The phone rang at dawn. "Hallie, it's me. Don't be mad. I can't leave for college if you're mad at me."

"I'm not mad, Flavia, I just feel rotten."

"I feel rottener. I thought it would be easier to go if I didn't miss you. Or Michael. I was mean on purpose. Hallie, I'm sorry. Somehow I tried to be farther away from you instead of closer. Kind of get an early start on being out of town, I guess. Hallie, don't be mad."

I said, lying, "I was just going to phone you anyway, Flavia."

"That makes me feel so much better. If I had to leave with a fight between us, it would be the worst possible start to college."

Even the end of our friendship was second to college. "What are you wearing?" I asked. Flavia and I could always discuss clothes.

"Jeans and a sweatshirt. I don't want to look too eager. If I get dressed up, I'll look hick."

I started sobbing. Flavia was still my best friend. I cared. I wanted it to be wonderful for her at Princeton.

"Come over, Hallie?" said Flavia. "Quick before we leave for the airport? The phone isn't good enough. I want to hug good-bye."

Jaz's Jaguar had two doors; his parents' Jag had four. Otherwise it was the same car. Oh, how I would miss driving in that wonderful car! Mr. and Mrs. Innes sat in the front seat. Jaz stood in the drive, waiting for me.

His belongings had been shipped. You don't load a Jaguar with coat hangers and laundry bags. Jaz had a wallet, a checkbook, and an American Express card. Period.

The tide was coming in. Waves smacked the breakwater like hands clapping. I won't cry, I told myself.

I. Will. Not. Cry.

Into my hand, Jaz pressed a tiny package. It was the size of a jeweler's ring box. It weighed almost nothing. Jaz's eyes were dancing. I held the ring box in my hand, disbelief and belief rising like tides, pressing against the dam I'd built up to keep from crying. *A ring?* Had he saved the real present for last? Although we had never talked about any future but his — any plans but college — did he have plans? Were they the same as mine?

"Open it, Helen Miranda," Jaz ordered.

I could not breathe, could not think. I tore the silver paper off, shredded the pink ribbons. The bare box was plain white, an inch square. I actually studied my left hand. "Jaz!" I whispered numbly. I opened the tiny lid.

It was a roll of stamps.

"Now you have to write me," Jaz cried. "No excuses." He kissed me, lips burning from the heat of his excitement. Adulthood, future, life, these three: waiting. "Bye, Hallie. I love you! Use my stamps! I'll telephone when I'm settled."

His father started the car. Jaz jumped in the back, rolled down his window, and leaned out, throwing kisses. "Keep the town under surveillance for me!"

I held the ring box of stamps.

"Good-bye, dear," said Mrs. Innes firmly, smiling a satisfied cat smile.

I stepped out of their path.

I was alone on the pebbles of the circular drive.

Weight crushed my chest so severely I had to sit. Like Henny Penny in the nursery rhyme. *The sky is falling, the sky is falling.* The weight of the universe had fallen on me.

Jaz is gone.

They're all gone.

Now what?

Eight

"St. James is looking for waitresses," Gloria said. "Mother! Don't I even get to sleep late a single day?"

"You've had all summer. Your friends are gone. Stop making excuses and find a job."

I drove slowly, taking back roads, changing radio stations every few seconds. None of them were playing anything decent. I hated having an empty seat next to me. What are cars for, if not company?

Waitressing. Oh, well, it would be something to do. St. James was a nice restaurant, nice clientele. I would take weekends, when tips were better. If I ran into anybody I knew, I would explain it was just temporary.

The hostess smiled as I walked in. "One?"

I glanced into the restaurant. It looked friendly enough. I could stand it for a while. "I'm not here to eat. I understand you're looking for waitresses."

Her eyes started with my hair and moved down,

checking my dimensions, clothing, posture. "What experience do you have?"

"None." People give me anything when I smile — substitute teachers, principals, neighbors. I smiled, thinking — I've charmed the tough ones, like Johnny D'Andrea. This is a piece of cake.

"We don't take beginners." She turned to a couple behind me. "Two? Come with me, please." They followed her to a table by the window, she poured ice water, and they all laughed.

I backed out of the restaurant. My cheeks hurt, as if my smile had bitten back. Turning me down! I ran the whole school, I can certainly waitress in your stupid restaurant! I coached my own cheerleading squad! You think I can't pour water? I'll never drive down this dumb road again. I hope St. James gets hit in a gale.

"If nobody's hiring waitresses, you could bus," Gloria said.

"Bus! Scraping dirty dishes? Mother!"

"If you're going to be a snob about work," Gloria said, "this isn't the town. There are no snob jobs in Westerly. That's one reason your friends chose college. They don't want to scrape dishes either. Make up your mind, Helen Miranda."

"I'll find a job," I said sulkily.

"Go to the Town Hall. They need a part-time clerk and you took typing, didn't you?"

"Sophomore year. I can't remember it anymore."

"Helen Miranda, what did you learn in high

school?" demanded my mother irritably. "What *can* you do, anyway?"

I slammed out of the house. What did she mean — what could I do? I could organize anybody to do anything! I could raise Spirit to ten times the level anybody else could! I could decorate any cafeteria to be the equal of any ballroom, that's what I could do.

Gloria, of course, has held any job that exists in Town Hall. "Hi," I said to the Town Clerk, "I'm Hallie Revness, Gloria's daughter." They have to give me this job, I thought, because they're friends of my mother's.

"Hallie, how nice!" She beamed at me. Everybody in the office beamed at me. It was a sunny, crowded place, four women and two men, phones ringing, typewriters clicking, computer screens blinking. I liked the feel of it. St. James was dumb old waitressing, I thought; it wasn't me. Business is me.

"Now fill out this application, Hallie, take the typing test, and then we'll talk."

I love forms. The only thing I regret about not going to college is that I would have liked to fill in all those pages of forms everybody else had. One of my hobbies is filling out book-club cards stuck in magazines. I wrote tons of answers and took my typing test, feeling pretty cheerful.

The Town Clerk said, "Hallie, honey, I'm going to be straight with you. Your form is rather sweet, the way you've filled it out, and being Editor of the yearbook and Varsity Cheerleader is fine, but that was high school. This is work. I'm afraid you should have left "experience" blank, because you don't have any. I'm rather surprised that you've never held a job of any kind."

The office was watching, heads cocked, like birds at a feeder. Bright little eyes and greedy little mouths. "We might still have given you a trial period, Hallie, but you failed the typing test. Now my suggestion is that you go to business classes in the evening, learn some basic skills; meanwhile get a low-level job, prove that you're responsible and reliable. That will make people more interested in hiring you."

I was numb. My lips were stiff, as if I'd had Novocain. I didn't say a word. I just barely managed to get out of the office, into the hall. From behind the door, their words followed me, "It's a shame the way children graduate from school these days and don't know how to do a thing. Gloria's daughter! Isn't that amazing?"

I drove to Gretchen's. She works evening shift so she's around by day. How tired Gretchen looked. Punctured, like a flat tire. Meg was napping on the living room rug. The house was grim and dismal, as if Gretchen cleaned with despair instead of Clorox. Gretchen turned off her soap opera. I pointed questioningly to Meg.

"Never move a sleeping baby, Helen. You'll want that rule for future reference."

"Mom wants me to get a job, not a baby. Talk to me about jobs, Gretch. Do you like your job?"

"How could anybody like my job? We make control panels for traffic lights. I stand in a line for eight hours, attaching blue wires to blue, and yellow wires to yellow."

"Why?"

"I take it you don't mean why yellow attaches to yellow." Gretchen stared at her sleeping baby. "Because it pays well. It has benefits. When Meg is sick, it pays the doctor bills and the drugs. I even have baby-sick days, which means I can stay home with her up to one week a year and still get paid."

"I can't do that."

"Of course you can. Any fool can. They're desperate for help. You can work any shift you want."

"I mean, with my life."

Gretchen laughed. It was a horrid laugh: more desperate for help than any assembly line. "How many choices does a person get with her life? I made lots of choices, but none of mine counted."

"Hallie! Fifty-six of us are sharing one hall phone! That's why it's been four days. I'm really sorry."

A thousand miles vanished. I pictured him leaning on some dim, poster-covered wall. "It's okay, Jaz. How's college?"

"I love it, Hallie. Orientation was a bunch of silly little exercises to break the ice, but fun, you know? I have a great group to eat with, and I know it's impossible to believe, but the cafeteria has great food."

His voice filled my soul. I wanted him to talk on and on. "Tell me about your roommates, Jaz."

"Charlie's from Iowa. Rob's from Florida. Classes haven't started yet, but I've bought my books. I've even done some reading. I'm especially excited about Chinese. You know how sure I am that China's going to open up to Western business the very day I graduate, and I want to be ready. I went in early to meet the professor, and she is wonderful, fascinating. We're already making plans for tutorials with grad students from China, because I'm not interested in learning to read Chinese, just speak it fluently."

China sounded remotely familiar, as if Jaz might have mentioned it once. I tried to remember anything about China. The Yangtze River came to mind, and a picture book about a duck called *Ping*. The people had no fashion sense, buried their ancient emperors with stone horses, and had a Great Wall somewhere. I didn't seem to have enough information to contribute to a discussion on China. Jaz discussed China like a news anchor. "It's going to be great, Hallie," Jaz concluded. "What are *you* doing? Found a job yet?"

"Jaz, you sound like my parents. It's only been four days." It felt like four months. As if Thanksgiving should be here any minute, Jaz flying home again.

He laughed. "Amazing, huh? I feel as if I've been here for weeks, it was so easy to fit in." How comfortable he sounded. Not like somebody standing in a hall, but curled on a soft sofa, half asleep. "When are your folks leaving on their big trip, Hallie?"

"They don't go till I get a job, and I'm not looking."

He laughed again. "I have to get off. There's a line of guys waiting their turns. Write me, okay?"

I clung to the phone. We had hardly started to talk. I had told him nothing. "Jaz," I said, trying to keep him.

"Love ya," he said. "Bye."

The evening went on.

Its shape was the shape of television: a half-hour show, a one-hour show; a long ad, a short ad.

I watched little television senior year; we were always out, always on the go. It was strange to be in front of a TV and have something other than my father's news on. Usually if I had the misfortune to be home during the evening, I was lying on my bed, with my best friends Radio and Telephone.

I went upstairs. High school covered my bedroom walls: posters and pompons, dried corsages, and candids I had not put in the yearbook. A museum. Close it up and a hundred years later people would stand behind a velvet rope and point.

I stood in the door myself, as if rope-blocked, when the phone rang.

"Hallie," shrieked Flavia, "how are you? College is *fab*ulous. Princeton is *won*derful!" Flavia, who never liked too much emphasis on anything, exaggerated each syllable. It made her sound like somebody else. "Before I left home, Hallie, I had spun the most involved daydreams. I really knew college could never be that terrific, but it's even *better*. Tonight we're having a boxer shorts contest. The one with the most vulgar shorts gets the most pizza. I wanted to call you before, but our phones are *always* out of order. It's so annoying. Liz and Kimmy and Vegas and I are getting our own phone, of course. Even the food is excellent. I'm worried about weight gain. You know — the famous freshman fifteen." Flavia chuckled.

Liz . . . Kimmy . . . Vegas . . . of course. In only four days she had reached that level? "What's the freshman fifteen?" It hadn't become famous till now.

"Fifteen pounds, of course. That's what you usually gain your first semester, because eating is the biggest activity. If I gain fifteen pounds, Hallie, I'm never coming home again." Flavia laughed gaily.

Never coming home again. I felt sick and queer. "How's your roommate?" I was nervous talking to my best friend.

"Las Vegas is going to be a challenge."

I was glad to hear this. "Is she right there?" I asked carefully.

"Sure."

"And it's not going so well?"

There was a burst of giggles, a snapping sound, and a new voice said clearly, "It's going fine, Hallie. But I was valedictorian at my high school, too, and Flavia and I are having a little difficulty with mutual decisions. But I'm kicking butt and Flavia is admitting my superiority."

More giggles and snaps. Four days and Flavia had

the new friend she had planned for. "We want you to visit, Hallie," Flavia said.

We! Consultation with the new friend was required before my visit could be scheduled?

"September is im*pos*sible," said Flavia, leaning on syllables. "There is so *much* scheduled. Vegas and I are *drown*ing. But October would be okay. So what's happening? What are you up to?"

It was still August. I had an empty calendar. An empty house. And she could not fit in a visit till October?

Everybody had said I would get letters and they were right: eleven in the first three weeks.

Even a letter from Brittany, whom I scarcely knew. *I'm homesick,* Brittany explained, *and since you're the only one there, I have to write you.*

Kyle sent a postcard. *Couldn't get Economics scheduled and ended up in Music Appreciation. Thought I'd spend the year getting blasted at beer parties and instead I'm going to learn Mozart.*

Susannah's letter opened origami-style into a winged butterfly. *Survived my flight, didn't admit to a soul I'd never been on a plane before. The campus is beautiful. We had as many AIDS orientation classes as we did for the library. All the girls are terrific. Of course I've known them only two weeks. But it feels like a lifetime. I love California. They kid me about being an uptight Easterner, so I am cutting loose.*

The days passed.

The letters arrived.

People were having pizza parties. Floor parties. Study parties. Fraternity parties. Sweater-exchange parties. Pre- and post-football game parties.

Valerie wrote to say she hated her roommate and was afraid she might commit a homicide, which would not look good on her transcript.

Max could see no point to the whole college venture and was staying only till the end of the semester, so his parents' money wouldn't be wasted, and then he was quitting.

Michael did not write. I asked Flavia on the phone if she had heard from him. "Sure, I called him," Flavia said. "He's having a ball. Plus he's in a coed dorm, and he met this girl the very first night of Orientation that he's crazy about."

Gloria pedaled her bike to nowhere.

Dad studied the news.

I watched a lot of television.

One night, I tried seven times before I finally reached Jaz on the hall phone. "I tried out for a play and didn't make it," Jaz told me, "but I signed on as Assistant Stage Manager."

"You didn't go out for drama at high school."

He laughed. "I went out for *you* at high school."

I said, "Who are you going out for now?"

"Hallie. Come on. Nobody. Plus, I already know I'm going to need grad school. I'm studying pretty hard. It's tough to study in the dorm, people are so noisy; so I spend a lot of time at the library. There are two girls in my Chinese class who are as interested as I am, and the three of us meet twice a week with a tutor. Keeps me busy."

"Tell me about the girls." I couldn't help it. I had to know.

Jaz, irritated, controlling it, said, "Their names are Samantha and Nick. Short for Nicole. Samantha's from Ann Arbor, she's a day student, and Nick's from Texas, fluent in Spanish, figures she'll be America's only English-Spanish-Chinese speaker." He laughed. "Nick's so funny. She's really good at language, Hallie. She can joke in Chinese already, and we only know about two hundred words."

I wanted to be busy, too. But there was nobody to be busy with, or for. "How's that geology class you were worried about?"

"Hallie, I just took geology because science courses are required, but I love it as much as Chinese. I'm sort of thinking that a geological engineer who speaks Chinese would be useful. Maybe I could find oil in Mongolia, or something."

The conversation stunned me. He might actually have been speaking Chinese for all I understood. Where had grad school come from? Geology, Chinese language? In high school, what Jaz had mostly been was romantic. In a school where boys' passions were limited to football, deer hunting, and trucks, he had been truly unusual. "I didn't know you were thinking about engineering at all," I said.

"I'm not," he teased, changing gears. "I'm thinking about you."

That did not confuse me! "Me, too, Jaz. Every waking minute."

"Listen, every guy on the floor is lined up to use the phone to call *their* girls. I gotta go."

And he went, into that new world I could not picture.

In high school, I knew what he wore; which games he played in gym; what experiments he did in lab. There was no texture of him now. No sight, no feel, no scent.

He could be laughing, studying, or running late. Taking a nap or attending a lecture. I would not know.

Each day I slept late.

By the time I got up, my parents were at work. The house was quiet, and dusty yellow, the way houses are in summer when nobody's home.

Time changed. It weighed more, lasted longer, and had become dark and thick, instead of light and airy.

I spent a long time dressing. I always wanted loads of time for dressing, but never had it. I used to have to bolt down the stairs and skip breakfast in order to get to school. Now I spent half an hour just choosing earrings.

I had never ended an evening before eleven. Now I couldn't even get one started. Was I supposed to go to a movie alone? Sit at McDonald's by myself? Rent my own video? Talk on the phone to my sister-in-law?

I hated my parents for being busy. Dad finished the news and went out with his bowling club. Mom finished supper and vanished to her meeting.

The only people left were losers, like Marcy, who was evidently not going back to Louisiana after all, because I kept running into her. Why Marcy, O Lord?

September fifth, and a beautiful day. I went to the beach.

I stepped over summer mothers. It was the last day for them.

High school kids were planning what to wear their first day of school. How I used to agonize over the first day, but never cared the second. How I cherished fresh, clean notebooks the first week, and then lost interest and wrote all over the covers.

The kids sat by class: This year's seniors did not mingle with this year's sophomores. Several said, "Hi, Hallie," and I said "Hi" back. I went to my usual stake and spread my towel. So much bare sand lay around it. Maine is not known for sand; Westerly has a small stretch reinforced each year by dumping sand from trucks. We always complain about how crowded it is.

It was no longer crowded.

Mothers discussed pediatricians.

Retirees discussed Florida departure schedules.

I couldn't bring myself to lie down on the all-alone towel. I wandered up to the concession to buy french fries. The window was blocked by giggling junior high kids learning how to flirt with lifeguards. I walked down the high-tide line to look for beach glass.

From their beach chairs, summer mothers eyed me.

Another time I'd have known they envied my figure, my life, and my boyfriend.

But I was alone. No girlfriend, no boyfriend, no couple, no crowd.

They pitied me.

I drove through the marina, planning to get a lemonade at the outdoor cafe. Another week and it would be closed for the season. Johnny D'Andrea was there having a Pepsi. "Hey, Hallie," he said cheerfully. He was wearing grimy jeans, a sweatshirt with the sleeves ripped off, and sneakers shredded almost down to the rubber sole and the laces. "Summer people are almost gone." He pointed to nearly empty parking lots. "Still weekend boaters around, of course. The real work begins now. Got to store and repair two hundred of their toys." He threw his empty can over five vacant picnic tables, neatly missing five sun umbrellas. There was a satisfying clink as the soda can joined a hundred others.

"Good aim," I complimented. I thought, maybe he'll stay for another Pepsi. Nobody else to share with. I can't get together for a doughnut and coffee Saturday morning with somebody a thousand miles away. Can't have cheese burritos Monday night. I had thought miles meant nothing. True love was all. But miles mean everything. There is no way to cross them.

Johnny beat on his chest, like Wayne. "Yep. A guy has to have some skill in life. See you around, Hallie." He grinned, saluted, and went back to work.

My sister-in-law Jen was home, of course; she's always home, Leighton and Emmett wrapped around her ankles. "How does anybody run a day-care?" Jen said. "Why aren't they insane? I'm amazed the *National Enquirer* has never headlined that. *Yet another daycare teacher placed in padded room*."

I was pretty close to the padded room stage myself. I had to have company. I didn't care how old they were. "May I have the boys? We'll go to the beach."

"Yes!" shrieked Jen. "I'll get the beach toys. Stay all afternoon. Keep them for the week. Boys — a treat! You're going with your Aunt Helen."

I sat with the summer mothers. Helped Leighton and Emmett build sand castles, dam up the tide, capture snails. Rinsed scary seaweed off tiny toes.

"Did you have fun?" Jen asked when I took them home.

"I loved it."

"That is so nice, Helen. When I was seventeen, I would have figured life was over if I had to spend the day baby-sitting."

Nine

Wayne called.

I was so thrilled to hear the phone ring you'd have thought it was God.

"Hey, Hallie," he said. "Hear you're doing nothing, too, like me. Wanna go to a hockey game? I got tickets for Friday night."

"I'd love to." Anything to get out of the house, to be with somebody, have some action. "We're just friends," I reminded him. "I'm still going with Jaz."

I almost heard Wayne shrug. "It won't last. I've watched three classes graduate high school. They think there's a generation gap but what there is, is a college canyon."

"Why, Wayne, that's very clever. College canyon. I like that."

"Thought I was too dumb to say anything clever, huh, Hallie?" He heard my blush as clearly as I heard his shrug. "Don't worry about it, Hallie. You're catalogued with me now. You skipped college, they figure God skipped giving you a brain. We'll go to the hockey game as friends, don't worry, you won't have anything to hide from Jaz. But I promise you, baby, he's hiding stuff from you."

I had to talk to Flavia. Had to ask what she thought. She would say "I told you so" but then, she had told me so. I didn't care what my parents said about the phone bill. I'm visiting her, I thought, fighting tears. I can't get all the way to Michigan, but I can get to New Jersey. Even if I've never driven farther than Sable Mall.

"Fourth floor," cried a flutelike voice.

"Is Flavia there?" I was shaking. I felt two years old.

The flute was capable of bellowing. "Flavia, phone for you!" Sounded like a former cheerleader to me.

"Flavia's out!" came down a Princeton hall. "Is it Richard?"

Flavia was expecting calls from somebody named Richard? A boy was interested in her and she had not called to tell me?

But she had new friends to talk to now. She didn't need me. I could actually hear somebody near the phone crunching potato chips. It was like listening to friendship.

Wayne had thickened around the waist. He wasn't playing sports anymore; he was watching other people play. He bought a tray of nachos, two large

Cokes, a large M&M's, and a foot-long hot dog with everything.

He settled happily into his seat, yelling hello all around. "Been going three seasons now," he explained. "I know everybody."

"That was a great fight last week, wasn't it?" said the girl in the seat behind us, leaning forward to sample some of our nachos.

"Terrific," agreed Wayne. "I love when they fight. Hallie, this is Deb."

"You Wayne's new girl? Welcome to the crowd. Where do you work?"

The organ began its time-climb, chords shivering upward to build suspense. The hockey players circled aimlessly on the ice.

"I don't have a job right now," I said.

"No? They let you go?" Deb nodded. "Economy's lousy. You know who's hiring? Eastern Boat. Go there. Lots of overtime hours."

The only thing worse than working in a submarine parts factory would be having to work extra hours in a submarine parts factory.

Wayne, Deb, and Deb's date leaped to their feet, yelling and shaking their fists, spilling M&M's. I didn't see anything to yell about.

Deb laughed at my expression. "We need action. Blood on the ice. What do they think we paid for? Peace on earth?"

Game over, we went to a food booth, where everybody had more hot dogs, nachos, and Coke, to discuss car payments and which players had had teeth knocked out.

Wayne drove me home. "That was great, wasn't it?" he said. "Wanna go for the rest of the season with me? It's no fun alone."

I actually considered it. He was right about one thing. Nothing is fun alone. On the other hand, I'd rather be dead than go for the rest of the season. "I guess I'd feel uncomfortable explaining that to Jaz," I managed to say.

Wayne laughed. "Yeah, well, once Jaz explains to you what he's up to, call me back. Offer stays open."

Still another day and all the long silent evening to fill.

I drove aimlessly. Past Flavia's house, past Susannah's. Past the high school. I recognized every car in the teachers' lot.

I don't want classes or quizzes. Don't want film strips or library research. None of it meant anything to me when I was there, and it doesn't mean anything to me now. I want halls of laughter. Cafeterias of friendship. Parking lots of gossip. Forty-six people, shouting . . . *party's at my house tonight . . . Hallie, you're coming, aren't you?*

I actually wept.

I drove in the bus turnaround and idled the car in front of the birch trees, where I could see the entrance but not be seen. I could go in. Lots of graduates come back. You have to tell everybody how you're doing. Yell at former teammates, kid former principals.

But a visit as early in the year as this would be pathetic. Proof I had nothing else to do.

I wanted to go in so badly I had to hang onto the steering wheel to stop myself.

I went to McDonald's and had a hamburger. A sign on the counter said, HELP WANTED. Lunch rush began. People behind the counter dumped frozen french fries into wire baskets, slapped cheese on meat, wrapped, bagged, poured, scurried.

I could not get up in the morning and spend the next eight hours doing that. I would rather be dead. But what else am I good for?

The hamburger tasted of panic.

Flavia and Jaz's lives stretched out so neatly: their schedules, their dorms, their vacations, their studies. But my life! It didn't stretch anywhere. It just lay around, doing nothing.

The car drove itself back to the high school.

No, I'm not going in.

The car drove itself into student parking. It turned itself off.

Maybe this is a sign, I thought. Once I get in the door, I'll have an answer, or a solution. Maybe the very same moment I visit, another person I've forgotten about will be visiting.

I adjusted my sweater as if it were my first day of school. It was a long cardigan: college-style, everything but the letter — and the college.

What door to use? Couldn't go through the art room the way we always did. Couldn't bang on the cafeteria door and expect my friends to open the fire exit for me.

I went in the front. Dr. Stefford saw me from his open office and waved. "Hallie! Back from college so soon?"

I was shocked. "I didn't go, remember?" I had run this school for four years. I had been Dr. Stefford's sidekick. He knew everything about me!

"Of course, I do now. It's a sad thing, Hallie, but we get scooped up in each successive class. Would you believe this year's senior class is already getting ready to apply? We have three applying for early admission, so we're already sweating."

I could think of nothing to say. I ran my fingers in my hair and fluffed it around my shoulders.

The dreaded question came. "So what are you up to, Hallie?"

"My parents are away for a few months, so I'm managing the house."

"Domestic skills never hurt anybody. Then what?"

"I don't know yet."

He nodded. "Well, listen, Hallie, you keep in touch. I wish I had more time to chat. You be sure to run down and say Hi to Mrs. Targlia; you were always a favorite of hers."

Mrs. Targlia teaches Italian and Spanish. I took French. Dr. Stefford went back into his office. The secretary said, "So, Hallie, have your mother and father left yet?"

"They're leaving this weekend."

"My, my," said the secretary. "Such an exciting trip." She looked at the other clerk for rescue. The other clerk obligingly said, "So, Hallie. Visited anybody on campus yet, honey?"

They're being kind. They feel sorry for me. This is friend-ish.

I can't visit classrooms. Once I leave, the teacher will say to her kids, "See? Yet another reason why you must go to college."

That's Hallie Revness.
She's the Prom Queen.
She runs this school!
Aren't she and Jaz gorgeous together?

"So what are you doing?" Jaz said. He had developed a slightly frantic voice with me; too bright.

"I went to work at Sea Storm."

"We used to eat there twice a week. My father was crazy about their menu. What's your job?"

"Nothing. I lasted a day and a half. I couldn't stand catering to wintertime summer people."

"I'm a wintertime summer person," he said.

"No, you're not. These are people who come for a Weekend Special. They were doing Italian Renaissance on my day and a half."

"Hey! Sounds like fun."

"It was awful. I was the gofer. I had to drive into the village and pick up a prescription for some woman who forgot hers. I had to listen to somebody else whine about how if they'd known it was going

100

to be cold and windy they wouldn't have come."

I hate people who whine. They should just join in, and be enthusiastic, like me in high school. Now I was the whiner. Champion whiner. Pretty soon I'd have to go on a whine diet.

Jaz's hall phone had a metal cord, which he'd thwonk against the phone box. The more he thwonked, the more tense he was. "I want you to be happy," Jaz said, thwonking rhythmically. "I feel so rotten when I talk to you."

Wonderful. Make your boyfriend feel rotten when he hears your voice. "You have a great schedule, don't you, Jaz?" I said wistfully. "It sounds like such fun."

"Hallie. Aren't you having any fun at all?"

I burst into tears. Jaz was horrified. "Hallie, don't cry," he protested. "Don't cry."

I cried.

"Who are your friends right now, Hallie? What are you doing all day?"

"I'm not doing anything. I don't know what to do."

"I feel so guilty having this terrific time when you're miserable. I hate even calling you because — " He corrected himself hastily. "I love talking to you, I just — "

"Hate calling me," I said. "Maybe if you'd stop asking me what I do all day the phone calls would be easier."

"What am I supposed to ask?" yelled Jaz. "What somebody *else* is doing all day?"

101

I wanted my old life. Jaz my boyfriend, Flavia my girlfriend, high school my arena. The old rhythms, in the old places. *Come back home! I want senior year back!*

Jaz didn't want it back. He'd forgotten it. By the end of September, six weeks into college, his senior year was not only history, it was *remote* history, peopled by half-remembered faces now living in other states.

If I said, "Remember how we used to . . ." he could hardly stand it. That was the past; he didn't care about the past.

Senior year, that I had built for us, and he didn't care.

It hurt me so much after phone calls I had to cry myself to sleep. But what did I want him to do? Pretend he wasn't at college? Fake that he was miserable, too? Fail and drop out?

I baby-sat for Leighton and Emmett so Royce and Jen could go to a movie. I baby-sat for Meg so Gretchen could go to the laundromat. I got to hug a lot of babies. Not the same as hugging Jaz.

If I admitted how awful it was, Jaz became incoherent with distress and guilt. The discrepancy between our lives dried up his speech.

But if I lied ("Everything's great, Jaz"), he wanted details. In what way was everything great? A job? New friends?

So with Jaz I could neither lie nor tell the truth.

* * *

October eleventh. Most of my friends had been gone seven or eight weeks. Mother and Dad were leaving.

I had thought it might not happen. In the end, Gloria and Dennis were not going to pack up, fill the tank, and drive away.

I was wrong.

Even Gretchen came to say good-bye, bringing Meg. Meg was wearing the prettiest little smocked dress, pale yellow with white lace. She held out her arms and shouted joyfully, "Granny!"

Gloria hasn't a gray hair, an extra ounce, or a wrinkle. Her clothes were plum and teal, with an art deco scarf. "Granny" did not fit. "You look about sixteen," Gretchen teased. "I bet they still card you at bars."

Meg's little arms wrapped around Gloria like ribbon around a present.

Hug me like that. Please, Mom.

Jen took photographs. Meg posed, trying out a wave, a smile, even a bow, and getting a love-laden round of applause with each.

"I'll miss you, Meggie," whispered my mother.

Miss *me*! I thought. Oh, Mom, say that to me!

But she wouldn't. She would only say, *Why didn't you get a job? What are you going to do all day long? What's the matter with you? You really annoy me, Helen Miranda. Now grow up.*

"Bring me presents?" Meg asked hopefully.

"Millions. We'll be back for Christmas. You put up an extra stocking."

I was afraid to hug Mom. Touching Gloria is always debatable. We had tiptoed around each other this final week, as if Gloria feared the Big Trip would literally be a Guilt Trip; that she'd drive across the country with as much guilt as gasoline in the tank. I felt as if I were keeping to the letter of the smallest small print of the most complex contract in the world.

I was overwhelmed by loss and fear. *Mommy, don't go!*

But if I said that, Gloria would just drive faster.

Derek pulled in. Royce walked Derek around back while Jen scooted Gretchen out the front to avoid confrontation. How sordid it was.

Gloria turned silent and cold. The chance to hug was gone; she was untouchable. How glad Gloria was to put Rocky Mountains and Great Lakes between us. She'd been listening to her children's problems for three decades. It was enough.

"Take care of Helen Miranda," Mom said.

"Of Hel?" Royce said. "She's the toughest of the bunch, Mom."

"Are you sure it's all right for her to stay with you, Jen?" my mother said.

"We adore Helen."

"Make her get a job," said my mother. "Now, Royce, you have the bank accounts, you have the dates on which to pay the bills. Keep the heat high enough so the pipes don't freeze. Don't forget to — "

"Mom!" said Royce. "I will pay the bills. I will

look out for Helen Miranda. I will make her get a job. She's seventeen, not some infant who can't take care of herself. Now go have a good time."

"Bye, Mommy," I said, tears sprouting like little plants. I could not risk a step toward her.

She came to me. Real arms, encircling, holding. She was solid and full of love. "You haven't called me Mommy in a hundred years," she said. I leaned on my mother desperately, but timed myself, knowing Gloria would withdraw if I overdid it. "Bye," I whispered, stepping back. "Drive carefully."

My mother actually stepped after me, to hug a second time. It was a Hurricane Gloria hug: The tempo of her life poured into that clenching, whole-body grip. Kissed me three times, once on the forehead, once on each cheek. "Bye, sweetie. Take care. Mommy and Daddy love you."

They got into the camper. Gloria was driving. "Symbolic," Royce said. "Mom figures Dad might turn around to catch the evening news if she doesn't make a lot of mileage the first day."

"What *is* he going to do about the news?" Jen said.

"Are you kidding? This man has a list of every radio station in the nation. He's in heaven. He'll have the news every hour on the hour, from here to Sacramento."

We made Leighton and Emmett wave. And then everybody but me had places to go, people to see, things to do.

* * *

I, who never walk anywhere, for whom a car is not transportation, but a party on wheels, front seat spilling with friends and talk and radio, parked my car and walked down the beach.

Clouds covered the sun.

A cruel damp wind flicked off the rough water.

Autumn passes quickly in the north. Winter was already coming.

A cardboard wrapper from a six-pack, a Styrofoam cup, and a single torn sneaker were all that remained of summer.

The party was truly over.

Ten

I stayed with Jen and Royce three nights. Then Royce said, "Craven's has an opening in the assembly line on the seven A.M. to three shift, Hallie. I signed you up."

Craven's? Where Gretchen worked? "This is a brother?" I said.

"This is also a son," Royce said. "I promised Mom and Dad you'd have a job, and you're not trying to get one, so I got it for you."

"At seven in the morning?" I yelled. "To fix my hair and my clothes right, I'd have to be up at five-thirty!"

"I'll set the alarm," Jen said. "And Gretchen said to be sure to wear your hair pulled back so it doesn't get caught in the machinery."

"I refuse to work around any machines that might grab my hair!"

"Well, what job have you gotten on your own?" they yelled.

So I got up at five-thirty. I hated being told how to wear my hair, but the vision of my black cloud ripped off my scalp made braids appealing. I put on dark green trousers, a really pretty shirt that I belted with a darker green rope, and spent a long time deciding on which earrings I liked most.

I got to Craven's at exactly seven.

"You the new girl?" said an angry-looking woman. "Revness, right?" I nodded. I wasn't late; what was she mad about? "Okay. You'll be training in wires. Follow me. Don't wear earrings again; no jewelry, it dangles. Dangling is dangerous. Wear a shirt you tuck in. It's greasy here, don't wear good clothing again. I gotta smock you can borrow." She handed me a repulsive short-sleeved cotton jacket in salmon pink. My green blouse sleeves stuck out from under the pink.

We walked into a room with ceilings as high as a gymnasium. So far across the vast room it blurred was huge machinery that clanged, whacked, and screamed.

Three women stood at a revolving table, attacking rectangular boards with pliers. Twisting wires, tossing boards, they worked steadily, yelling back and forth. One was fat and frumpy, her hair hidden by a torn bandanna. Her thin bony companion chewed a huge wad of gum. The third was Julie Canova, who graduated with Wayne. Julie was delighted to see me. "Life's one big cheerleading routine for Hallie!" she yelled to the others.

The thin woman transferred her gum to the opposite cheek. She finished one board and set it down; the table swung. She picked up the next, jerked right with her pliers, flipped the board like a baton twirler, and repeated the twists twice more. She set it down, the table swung again, and more panels were spit out of an opening to her right.

The room hammered and screamed. Julie lifted a board to show me what to do. Jaz and Flavia still had the old life. By day they had more high school and by night, endless slumber parties. And I was supposed to spend my life screaming to be heard, twisting wires around little knobs?

"No! I can't do this! I'm going. Thank you, anyway. I'm sorry." I ran. I ran out of the room, ripping off the horrid smock and dropping it on a chair outside the angry woman's office. No wonder she was in a bad mood. Who could ever smile again with that life? I ran out of the building; I almost ran past my car. I drove around for hours. Flavia had said my ego was so big it would balloon over the Atlantic. I had said conceit was a wonderful thing, and I had plenty. What a pathetic joke.

Jen fixed a pot roast with oven-browned potatoes, gravy, and biscuits with honey. Now I knew why men with tough jobs demanded meals like that. There had to be something warm and good in life.

"So how was the first day of work, Helen?"

I could fake it. Just drive away at quarter to seven every morning, pretending . . . oh, right. And just where was I going to go? The beach — in winter?

McDonald's, for the next eight hours? "I didn't stay. It was too awful. I can't do that."

Royce and Jen yelled at me for hours. "What do you think life is about?" Royce said sternly. Royce, mind you, who once thought life was about skipping school, driving fast, and turning up the radio.

"If that's life, that horrible room, with that noise, and the grease, forget it! I like things to be neat. And I like nice clothes. And I want to be with kids my age. And have friends. And laugh a lot."

"If that's what you want, go to college," said Royce. "Nothing else shelters you from the real world, Helen."

We glared down into our pot roast and gravy. Emmett, toddler sympathy aglow, was eager to identify my problem. "Aunt Helen? Bad day?"

"Bad life," I snapped at him.

"Alternatively," Jen said, "how about a job that isn't messy? Where you get to wear pretty clothes? You could clerk. How about the department stores at Sable Mall?"

I refused to go, so the next day Jen got a babysitter and drove me. We walked through Filene's, Lord & Taylor's, Sears, and Montgomery Ward's. Jen kept pointing to the PERSONNEL signs. I kept saying, "But all clerks do is arrange clothes on racks. I hate clerks when I go shopping. They're always after you to buy instead of look."

"Just apply," said Jen.

"No."

So we went home. I lay on the floor with Leighton and Emmett. We sang with Mr. Rogers and did our numbers with *Sesame Street*.

Jen made lasagne — deep layers of sausage and mozzarella and spicy tomato sauce. "Helen," my brother said, "if you're not going to work, you're not going to be a welcome guest. Here's my wife slaving away raising two kids and making the meals and you're just sponging off her."

I used to be a daughter who lived with her parents. Now I was a sponge. I was nothing, other people were slaves. Jaz and Flavia got to go right on sponging; their parents were even paying tens of thousands of dollars so they could sponge four more years.

"Fine," I said, spitting it out. "I'll move back to my own house. I'll cook my own meals. I don't need you." I left the table, left my lasagne, and went upstairs for my toothbrush.

"You can't do this," Royce said. "Mom and Dad said for you to stay with us."

Jen blocked the door. "Your clothes are here," she pointed out. "You've sent all your friends our telephone number, and — "

"And they haven't phoned, have they? I'll call them from Mother and Daddy's. And my clothes are not all here. I have millions of clothes. I moved one suitcase over here."

"Your mother and father will telephone to check," Jen said nervously. "What am I supposed to say?"

"Say I'm old enough to make my own decisions, and I've decided not to work in a factory, and I've decided not to live with you."

Royce shrugged. "Okay. Check in now and then, though."

"Royce! You can't let her! She's seventeen."

"She knows how to lock a door, Jen. She knows how to make macaroni and cheese. Anyway, she'll be back. This is my sister, the party animal. Think she can be alone more than twenty-four hours? Just don't throw any wild parties, Helen Miranda. No wrecked furniture."

"I don't know a single person anymore. I don't have a single friend. What do you think I'm going to do," I screamed, stomping out of the house, stomping to the car, "put up a sign on the interstate asking tourists to come to my party?"

Our house had been stuffed with people: boys who raised hell, a mother pedaling furiously to no-where, a daughter on the phone, a car horn beeping Morse code, a party starting. Television had wrapped us in a cocoon of internationally known voices (. . . *and in the news tonight, East Germany* . . .).

In this house, nothing happened. Nobody spoke. Nobody cooked. Nobody visited.

The house developed thickness, as if the atmosphere had literally changed. It was full of its own emptiness. Echoed its own soundlessness.

I was not afraid.

I was suspended.

Time became a physical thing: as visible and heavy as fieldstone.

My parents were not happy about it.

"Helen Miranda, what did you think would happen after high school, anyway?" my father said. "I mean, how did you picture this?"

"I don't know."

My mother said, "That won't accomplish anything, Dennis. Now, Helen, I want you to move back with Royce and Jen. I don't want you alone in the house."

"I'm seventeen and a half, Mother. There hasn't been a burglary in this neighborhood in my lifetime. The neighbors know I'm here. Royce calls every night. Last night I went back and had supper with them and baby-sat the boys."

"Well, turn the heat back up," my mother said irritably. "I don't want you to freeze."

I had turned the heat back up the minute I walked in the door. I had also charged a whole lot of groceries. In a small town, you can charge anything, weeks on end, and nobody thinks twice about it.

"Do you have any money?" my father asked mildly.

"Yes. I have my five hundred dollars graduation money."

"Spent any yet?"

"Some." It terrified me how quickly the money was vanishing. One trip to the drug store for necessities and thirty dollars was swallowed. A week of lunches out and another thirty was gone. A pretty sweater to make myself feel better and seventy-five vanished.

"We'll call every other night," my mother said. "At dinnertime. You be there to answer that call, Helen Miranda."

How I missed talk!

Silence is awful. I left the television on all day, all night, just to have conversation. Pretend conversation! Memorized, script conversation! But voices all the same — laughing, gossiping, arguing, informing.

When he phoned, Jaz listed what he'd done all day. He listed what his friends had done all day. I had no lists to match. "Why aren't you happy?" he said. "Everything is your own choice."

"I don't know what to do."

"Don't cry. Please don't cry."

In another life, in high school, we shared a front-page flirtation. What I had now with Jaz was not romance. He was scraping me up with a spatula.

Thwonking the phone cord against the wall, so that every other syllable was metallically empha-sized, Jaz tried to find a subject for us. "The uni-versity is organizing a trip to China. Several trips, actually, but the one Samantha and Nick and I are interested in goes in July. Not much sight-seeing. Mostly studying; we'd stay in Beijing, attend classes, observe." He sighed, filling a stranger in on the details everybody else already knew.

He doesn't want a cheerleader, I thought. Stuffed with fluff like Winnie the Pooh. He wants Samantha or Nick.

"And in geology, I'm doing a research paper that really interests me." He sighed again.

There was nothing that really interested me. There was not a thing for me to say. Because I was no longer interesting either.

"Hallie, remember how I signed up as Assistant Stage Manager? Well, the production is opening and I'll be busy every night for a couple of weeks. I won't be able to phone."

Eleven

Flavia wanted me to come midweek instead of the weekend. "It'll give you a better feeling for college life," she insisted.

"I don't want a feeling for college life, I just want to visit you."

"So visit me Tuesday through Thursday."

"You have weekend parties you don't want me at, Flavia?"

"Hallie! How could you! I seriously want you to experience college."

"I seriously don't."

Flavia said nothing for a while. Then, "Listen, I miss you. Come whenever you want. You tell me, I'll be here."

"Pay attention," yelled Derek. "I rotated the tires, checked the brakes, changed the oil, everything's fine." It irritated me that Derek was showing up after all these months and being a White Knight. Why couldn't he be a White Knight for Gretchen and Meg? Derek gave me fifty dollars with no restrictions on spending, which was nice. Royce had given me a hundred for emergencies with strict orders not to spend a cent; he needed it to buy the boys snowsuits. "Now do you know how to get there?" yelled Derek. "Stay on the interstates."

"Stop worrying about me, Derek. Worry about Meg and Gretchen instead."

"Hallie, they're fine," my brother said, which goes to show there are at least two definitions of "fine."

I thought I would never get there. We're so far north. I had not known I had a fear of intersections or a horror of merging until I hit Real Traffic, meaning all the way from Boston to New Jersey. When I finally reached Flavia's dorm, the parking was at the bottom of a steep hill. At least it wasn't parallel parking, proving there are still some good things in a difficult world.

Every girl wore a very long, dark coat. My ski jacket was wrong. Even my jeans were wrong. Nobody was wearing jeans. How could blue jeans be wrong anywhere in America?

But Flavia hurled herself on top of me. "Hallie, I've been watching from the window! I thought you'd be here hours ago! Was the traffic horrible? Oh, God, you look super, you look terrific, I'm so glad to see you, God, I love your hair like that. And I forgot about your swear diet, I take all the gods back."

Somebody was glad to see me. Oh, how long it had been! "I thought I would be killed coming through New York City," I said. "Nobody told me that I have never really seen traffic before."

"You're one up on me," said Flavia. "I flew down. I could never drive through that, never." She hugged me again. My first hugs in weeks from anybody over two years old.

We walked up three flights and into a room that was stupifyingly messy, strewn with makeup, jewelry, discarded clothing, books, cassettes, and cookie boxes. From under a black puff on the upper bunk emerged a tiny face surrounded by red curls. "Hallie!" cried Vegas. "We've heard so much about you!" Vegas vaulted off her bunk, landing on and crunching something. "We planned to celebrate your arrival," Vegas said, "but you're late, and we already ate and drank the celebration." She twinkled at me. I liked her.

Flavia had the bottom bunk, which she cleared by jerking the blankets until everything on the bed hit the floor. We curled up on her bunk, Vegas kicked an opening on the floor, dropped her pillow on the opening, and her bottom on the pillow.

From under a pair of corduroy trousers, Vegas took crackers, and from under the bed, a jar of peanut butter. There was no knife, so Vegas used a fingertip to scoop out peanut butter and spread it on the crackers. "We lost all standards in about forty-eight hours," she confided.

I giggled insanely. The peanut butter on crackers was dry enough to gag a camel. I wanted Vegas to like me; it was a weird feeling. I felt like pitiful Marcy

118

Hampson in the halls; please, please, please, don't just be "friend-ish."

Kim bounded in. "This is Hallie?" she said happily. "I'm so glad to meet you, Hallie. Welcome to Princeton. I see that Vegas and Flavia are being revolting as usual. Scraping food up off the floor. Luckily, I have a little class."

The party extended out onto the hall carpet and enveloped the pay phone. Everybody had a pillow or blanket, radios played, somebody was on the pay phone the whole time, and behind closed doors somebody kept yelling, "Shut up so I can study!"

Nobody shut up.

We ordered nachos, pizza, and grinders and ate some of every order.

The girls leaped from subject to subject: They covered the morality of wearing fur coats, race relations on campus, the possibility of a junior year abroad, the word count of required papers, and the weather in New Jersey.

"You haven't mentioned boys," I said at last. "Here you are with thousands of choices walking around you, and nobody is grading bodies or coming up with strategies for attracting male attention."

Everybody giggled. "We're trying to impress you," Vegas said. "We want you to think we're intellectual and academic."

"A lot of the boys are brain dead," Flavia said. "Or ugly. Or gay. Or taken."

"Or jocks," Vegas said. "Every time I fall in love with some gorgeous mountain of a guy, I see him in the cafeteria eating like a mechanized shovel, saying things like, *Uhnnh,* or *Bzlmk*."

"I adore Robbie," Kim said, "but Robbie's going to medical school and has to get straight A's. He says it isn't possible to do that and date at the same time. I say we should at least try. He says he doesn't like a pushy, demanding woman. Then there's this boy in my economics lecture whom I worship from afar. I haven't even found out his name yet, but he has hair like yours, Hallie, great black waves I'm yearning to possess."

In the morning, Flavia had Chaucer at 8 A.M. and they discussed "The Pardoner's Tale." Many things do not interest me at eight in the morning, and Chaucer is one.

Then chemistry lecture. Hundreds of students. "So far," whispered Flavia, "it's nothing we didn't have in high school. You could do this."

Oh, right. I who learned enough chemistry each night to get through the following day and now remember absolutely nothing except that I sat by the window.

From there we hiked over the campus for lunch. "It's all perfect, isn't it, Flavia?" I said.

"Perfect if you like compromise. Take my roommate. Vegas is nauseatingly messy. And she borrows my clothes and stretches my sweaters and uses up my shampoo and charges calls to my phone card. But we have to get along. So I laugh it off."

The day was a blizzard of lectures, labs, activities.

How beautiful a schedule is. If you don't have one, every long ghastly minute of life whispers, *now what? now what? now what? now what?* until you go insane from the answer *now nothing, now nothing, now nothing.*

"You know what Princeton reminds me of, Flavia? Meg's nursery school."

"What?"

Something terribly important was coming to the surface; I was about to stumble on something I needed. "Now we go to class; now we cross the campus; now we eat together using meal cards; and now we have playtime in the dorm. Now we go to the library; now we have profound discussions; now we have quiet time."

Flavia was outraged. "We are very independent. We make our own choices."

"You choose whether to have cereal or eggs for breakfast. But it's handed to you."

"Of course it's handed to you! This is college."

"I'm not trying to pick a fight, Flavia. I'm just trying to think things out. This is another home. Furnished rooms, furnished meals, housekeepers, classes and activities laid out. Sheltered. I hadn't realized how contained it would be. They're keeping you cozy and safe for another four years."

Flavia could hardly breathe. "It's very demanding, Hallie. We are under tremendous pressure, academically and socially."

"Do you really think so? I mean, consider Orrin."

"Orrin?"

"I had to get him his yearbook. He dropped out of high school to work the night shift because his mother couldn't even pay the utility bills. Orrin talked to all the armed services and chose the Navy. He's in training and sending his mother the money to — "

"Hallie, I cannot believe you are comparing Princeton to joining the Navy. I can't understand, except you must be so bitter. You'll throw any old mud to make yourself feel better about your own dumb decision."

"Orrin's working harder than" — I corrected myself — "I mean *as hard as* college kids. Talk about pressure, he can't spend a cent; he's sending it all home, and *his* four years — "

"Hallie."

"Okay. I'm sorry."

"You're not really sorry. You came all this way just to spit that out."

"I didn't, Flavia. I didn't even think this till now. Don't be mad."

Flavia was mad.

I said, "How come you're the only one who can have profound thoughts? I'm not going to college so I'm not allowed to think anymore? I'm the one facing the world. Flavia, what have you learned about time, and loneliness, and jobs wiring control panels? What do you know of sleeping late to spare yourself the agony of being awake? What do you know of friend-ish secretaries?"

Princeton was so beautiful. It was like a resort: like Sea Storm.

"I do see, Hallie. I feel how empty the house is, how long the days are. But there's such a simple solution. Go to college yourself. What have I been telling you all along?"

"But I don't want any more school. I want some other life, but I can't see it. Orrin is lucky. He sure has a purpose in life."

"My purpose is getting a college education," said Flavia.

"But that's just another four years of protection from the real world."

"I hate that word *real*," Flavia said. "My life is more real than yours. You haven't done a thing in weeks except drive around the block and mope."

We sat on a bench, looking across a campus flaming with autumn colors. "You're right," I said wearily. "Flavia, Jaz is sick of me. What am I going to do?"

"Fly out and see him."

"No money."

"What's he sick of, exactly?" Flavia said at last.

"My phone calls. I'm dreary. I have nothing to say. And he's surrounded by people with a million things to say. Interesting people."

"You're interesting," Flavia said.

"I *was* interesting. Flavia, do you think Jaz and I truly loved each other? Or did we just love having romance during senior year?"

She shook her head. If she knew the answer, she also knew better than to say it.

"Who's Richard?" I asked. "Is he some boy you like?"

She laughed. "He's some boy I *don't* like. I have to be friend-ish to him, Hallie. No, nobody seems to date here. We hang out, we go in groups, we meet each other places, but we don't actually go on dates."

"Are you sorry?"

"Not yet. I enjoy having a lot of friends. But one day I'll be sorry, I think. One day I'll want a single person to call, just for me, just to hear my voice, and if there isn't a person like that . . ." Flavia stood up. "Come on. It's getting cold. Let's go in."

"Flavia told us about how you decided not to go to college," said Vegas, "and I understand perfectly. My best friend is spending a year in France first. She wants to be totally fluent before she starts college. And I have another friend who is on the *verge*, the very *edge*, of breaking into Broadway. Here, look at a photograph of her on stage. So I absolutely understand. What exactly are you accomplishing this year instead, Hallie?"

"Nothing. I'm just not going to college."

"I mean, when you *do* go to college," said Vegas, "what will you be doing? And what college do you think you'll attend?"

"I'm not going ever. It doesn't interest me."

"That's — neat," said Vegas dubiously. "Sort of a

124

sixties attitude, huh? You're going to do self-education? Maybe get into stuff like ecology?"

"Hallie," said Flavia, grinning, "is untainted by subjects like ecology."

"Oh. Well, downstairs tonight I've arranged for a slide show and lecture on the current situation in South Africa. Come on. We'll be late."

The only thing I know about South Africa is that it fills up the bottom of its continent. After the lecture, people asked my opinion. I didn't have one. "She's not interested in politics," said Flavia defensively.

"Hallie, what *are* you interested in?" Vegas asked, clearly planning to cater to my interests, which was thoughtful, but I had none.

The second night was not half as much fun. Whatever her friends said, Flavia had to translate for me. "He's a professor of anthropology." "He's a guy on the football team, has the brains of a house plant." Every discussion had to be outlined for me . . . every joke mapped.

Vegas told stories without explanations. "And then you should have seen Pepper," Vegas said. "Honestly! Pepper!"

Everybody laughed.

"Pepper's this truly weird girl," Flavia explained, enjoying the story. "She wears a trench coat with nothing under it."

"You're exaggerating, Flavia," Vegas said. "She wears a bra and pants under it."

"Where I come from, that's nothing."

"Yeah, but you come from a nothing place," Vegas said.

Everybody laughed.

Anger rocketed through me. I hated them. Snobby, awful, worthless —

Vegas said, in a pinprick of a voice, "So, Hallie, I hear you think going to Princeton is like going to nursery school."

Silence gathered like a storm, awaiting explanation.

"I'm just comparing my life with yours," I said lamely.

Vegas's mouth actually fell open. Even her eyes seemed to fall open, as if she could move her lower lids as well. Then she began laughing. She laughed so hard she slid off the lower bunk and lay upside down. "Oh, Flavia!" she said, tears of laughter falling backwards. "I'm sorry, I've tried to be polite, I know she's your best friend, but all I can say is, it certainly shows how few there were to pick from."

I have to give Flavia credit.

Flavia threw them out, even Vegas, who lived there. When we were alone in the room, and Vegas's laughter faded on down the hall, Flavia began to cry. She put her arms around me. "What's happened to us? Oh, Hallie, I feel as if the San Andreas Fault opened between us. We've earthquaked."

To admit the quake healed it. The years of our friendship surpassed anything Vegas or Liz or Kim could supply.

"Wayne calls it the College Canyon," I said, sharing. That's what's missing, I thought: sharing. To be in school is to share all. To be out of school is to be alone.

Flavia's arms dropped. "*Wayne?* You are hanging out with Wayne? A pizza delivery man? Oh, my God, Hallie, what's going to become of you?"

Twelve

My parents sent armloads of postcards. On each Gloria wrote, "Having a wonderful time. People so friendly. Miss you. Love Mother and Daddy." They taped commentaries on the area they were driving through and mailed the cassettes. I had enough tapes to do travelogues.

They phoned on schedule. They would say, "How are you doing, sweetie?" and I would say, "Great! How's the Mississippi River?" I had thought the Mississippi River was around New Orleans, full of paddle-wheel boats. What a surprise to find the Mississippi all over the place, way up in Minnesota and Wisconsin. It seemed that postcards were produced to commemorate every mile of it.

None of the postcards awakened any travel lust in me. Not even when they reached California and sent cards of San Francisco, Los Angeles, and San Diego. I didn't want to go anywhere or do anything.

Although I fled the assembly line partly because

of clothes, I stopped caring about what I wore, as if I really were in a factory. I put on any old thing and didn't look at myself in the mirror before I left.

I hung out at Sable Mall. At least there were people around. One terrible afternoon I saw myself in a mirror. Old jeans, old sweatshirt, three shopping bags.

A junior bag lady.

I hid in the ladies' room at Sears, trying to regain control. I had a raging desire to take the nail file out of my purse and scratch my name onto the metal door. Anything to be somebody. When I staggered out, mirrors were everywhere, reflecting me, the mess, the failure.

In spite of how well I know Sable Mall, I could not find the exit. Mirrors forced me inward, back to more stores, more mirrors. Back to where Marcy Hampson was looking at sweaters. I greeted her with such a shower of delight it was all but rain. "Marcy! Hi! How are you? Gosh, how great to see you!"

Marcy gave me a measured look. "Hello, Hallie."

"Those are lovely sweaters. That color is really nice. I'm going down to the Food Halls. Want to get an Orange Julius with me?"

"No," Marcy said, moving on to another sweater stack.

I was so desperate that I actually said aloud, "I'd love some company."

Marcy laughed. "I could have used company a few times in the last two years myself, Helen Miranda Revness. But you and your precious crowd spent those two years forcing yourselves to be *friend-ish*."

Guilt surfaced like dirt through my pores.

She didn't stalk off; I didn't matter enough. She moved a few inches to another sweater display.

I dragged myself to the Food Halls anyway, as if it would prove something to Marcy. The smells made me gag, but lots of people sat alone, I wasn't conspicuous. Each tiny counter — pizza, yogurt, baked potatos, ribs, Mexican — had a sign: HELP WANTED.

I arranged my "Finest Longest Fries on Earth" in a row, planning to pick the finest and longest. A high school graduate has to have a skill, right?

A finger drilled in my spine like a gun.

I spun around, nerves so shot I actually expected a crazed mugger wanting my longest french fry.

It was Rand Willems.

Rand graduated two years ago, in Wayne's class. He's half and half, like coffee cream: his mother a rich summer person, and his father a swamp Yankee, so inbred Rand should have been born with six fingers per hand. What made them marry was anybody's guess. And Rand himself is jagged shards of each parent; you never know which piece will emerge — only that it will be the wrong one at the wrong time. He is handsome as a panther is handsome, going for the kill.

"Hey, pretty Hallie," he said. He grinned like a shark, tiny teeth stabbing behind narrow lips.

"Hi, Rand, how are you?" I was afraid of him. My pulse began racing out of control, a car without

130

steering. I could imagine his opaque eyes watching anything. Imagine his long bent fingers doing anything.

"Just out of jail," Rand said. He pulled his lips together like the edge of a package, to see what I would do.

"Welcome home. You going straight now?"

"Too boring. I have a responsibility to the old home place, you know. Got to keep it hopping."

"You're doing better than I am if you can keep this place hopping."

The finger that had stabbed my back now traced a circle around my face, curling under my chin, stopping in the middle of my forehead where he pretended to drill into my brain.

"Come with me," he said softly. "I'll show you some fun."

Wonderful to be the passenger in a boy's car again! The town might be emptied like a jar, old friends poured out into campuses, but there was still life.

I'm too young to get in a bar, but so's he; he had an assortment of fake IDs. He was willing to drive a hundred miles to find a bar that wouldn't look closely. But he preferred to stay in town. At first I could not understand: everybody knew him. Then I realized that was the point: everybody knew him.

Everybody on the edge when he walked in. Waiting, wondering, worrying about what Rand Willems would do.

Fear turned out to be romantic. Any raised pulse is as quick as one raised by love.

Wonderful to think again about what to wear. Even Jaz had been confused by clothing; I'd gotten my clothing attention from Flavia. But Rand would say, "I love how you tied that scarf, Hallie. Sexy."

When his mother's side of the family was showing, he liked to blend in with the rich yachties. When his father's side was showing, he might do anything. He simmered, heat just below the surface, as if his blood were over a gas flame. Peel back his skin and find glowing embers.

And oh! how I wanted to peel him back. "Remember, I'm really dating Jaz," I said every time he picked me up.

"And I'm really dating the First Lady," said Rand, using the swear words I'd given up.

I was like a blender with buttons. Rand pushed my button and I raced at whatever speed he picked. "Why'd you get kicked out of prep school?" I asked. Rand had been kicked out of quite a list of boarding schools.

"Parents would come visit their kids. They'd be driving the greatest cars. Probably rented to show off for the weekend. Ferrari or Lamborghini or Maserati. Every parent had to be flashier than all the other parents. It was a bore. You had to do something for excitement at those dumb schools. So I'd filch their keys and go for a spin."

"They didn't arrest you?"

"Course not. A parent's going to bring charges against his own kid's roomie? Nah. They just write it off to high spirits. The richer you are, the more high spirited you're allowed to be."

He intoxicated me. The word has "toxin" in it. Poison.

Rand embarked on a long story about how last summer his hobby had been sending distress signals to the Coast Guard so they'd have to rescue him at sea. "They never responded," he said. "Made me really mad. They'd call local rescue services, and there aren't enough of 'em boat-trained, and you'd sit out there in the water two, three hours, before anybody got to you. What if it was a real distress? People would drown, you know what I mean?"

I told Rand I wouldn't go out with him again.

But after I'd spent the day not going to the mall, not using Leighton and Emmett as substitutes for friends, and not getting any mail, I didn't care.

I went with him.

By the end of two weeks, I knew, and he knew, that I'd do anything he asked. It was a matter of when he felt like asking, and how much he asked for.

He loved to immobilize me. When we argued, he'd run his separated fingers into my hair and make fists. It hurt, like being scalped.

I did not kiss Rand, telling myself that as long as I didn't kiss him it wasn't a date, didn't involve Jaz.

So Rand kissed me. And I loved it. I can't deny it. It was warmth, it was need, and it was not hundreds of miles away studying Chinese.

Saturday afternoon we drove through the marina. I was nervous. Rand had just found out I was living alone. No brothers, no parents. "Alone," he repeated, chuckling to himself. "Well, well. That makes the evening much more interesting."

I slumped down. I did not want Johnny D'Andrea to see me with Rand. Not that I cared about Johnny's opinion. Flavia had been right about him, really. All that would happen in Johnny's life was changing the spark plugs on somebody else's motor. Still.

"What's that matter, you think I'm going to steal a boat?" He laughed.

Immediately I knew he was going to steal a boat.

Although it was November, too rough for pleasure sailing, there were still plenty of boats in the water. The marina was probably as understaffed as McDonald's. The workers were down beyond the cafe (closed now for the season) running an enormous hoist crane over a yacht being taken out of the water.

Rand drove slowly, staring at every moored boat. He stopped in front of the most dramatic yacht there. Too long to be in a vertical slip like the boats of ordinary sailors, it lay lengthwise: sleekly curved white hull with two slender stripes of dark crimson. Graceful as a scimitar. Cruel as modern weapons: a missile. Inside, the cabins would be pure luxury, rich fabrics, gleaming tropical woods.

"Let's spend the night on that," said Rand. "*The*

134

Arrogant. Isn't that typical? Who would name a boat that? We'll play with their rich boy's toy and they won't be so arrogant."

"Don't be ridiculous, Rand."

Rand parked. He circled the car like a soldier closing in, and opened my door, pulling me out. I ducked my head to escape his metallic eyes, but he took my hair, holding it tight in his fists. "Go on, swear at me," he whispered.

He could raise my pulse just by talking. I was thinner than I'd ever been. Shivers of desire used up calories. Or perhaps it was fear rather than desire: What if I lost control and went along with him?

Rand stepped onto the deck of the yacht. Its surface was pure gloss. "Virgin territory," said Rand, his shark teeth showing. "Perfect for you, honey. Come on board. We'll have fun."

The racket of the marina pummeled my thoughts. Straddle cranes and forklifts, slapping rigging and flags, power tools reverberating inside metal sheds, doors slamming. It reminded me of the factory; but it was not an indoor hell. It was wild, like hurricanes. Clean, like the wind off the sea.

I walked away from *The Arrogant*, leaving him on its white deck. I did not get in his car. I was afraid of the car. He would drive too fast. I couldn't get out unless he let me.

Rand leaped lightly off *The Arrogant*. He fell in step with me, mimicking my stride rather than matching it. We walked on to another pier, where a row of Cigarettes lay waiting their turn to be lifted out of the water. Cigarettes could hit seventy, eighty, supposedly ninety miles an hour. Strapped into semistanding protection like babies in molded car-seats, passengers flew over the water, slapping the waves with a violence that threatened to separate the brain from its wrappings.

Rand's brain had been detached from its wrappings long ago.

But who else is there? I thought numbly. Wayne? Jaz, twice a year?

Rand boarded a Cigarette and began assessing the controls. It took a key to start that kind of boat. He didn't have one. I didn't think he had one. You never knew with Rand. "They'll prosecute," I whispered. "Johnny D'Andrea's father is the manager. Get off the boat, Rand!"

Rand merely smiled. "Coming?" he said lazily. He fondled the boat like an owner. Like a lover. "Joy-riding's more fun than owning."

In some circles, joyriding is known as stealing.

Lennox, my graduating class's number-one scum, had found something to do in this town. He had robbed the Quik Stop. I, too, could find occupation. Although jail is not widely known as the first step toward success. Mrs. Land would send Flavia a clipping of the arrest. For Flavia to share with Vegas. Susannah in California and Michael in Pennsyvania would read about it.

And Jaz.

Remember that, I told myself. You love Jaz. He loves you. Hold that.

"I guess no, Rand." I backed away.

"You got no ride home!" shouted Rand.

"I'll walk."

"You can't walk no four miles!" yelled Rand.

Why did he have to shout? Somebody from the marina would come. He'd be caught. We'd both be caught. My insides writhed. My head ached. I wanted to go home, I wanted my mother.

"Get back here!" ordered Rand. He got out of the Cigarette and came after me. "Where you think you're going?"

I ran through the racks where the littlest boats were piled, past the empty playground, and the shuttered cafe. Rand got into his car, pressing the horn down in one long evil honk, and drove after me. I had the impression he would drive right through the boats to reach me. I ran one way, and then the other, while the horn blasted on and on.

Mr. D'Andrea came out of a metal building. "Hello, Helen," he said pleasantly. "I think I'll give you a ride home. I've asked the police to come and suggest to Rand that he is not welcome at the marina."

I was afraid I would cry.

Mr. D'Andrea said, "Helen, honey, I like your mom. She wouldn't want you running around with Rand Willems. Fact, now I think of it, you might spend the next few nights with your brother instead of being home alone. Your mom reach the Pacific Ocean yet?"

They all asked after my mother. Nobody asked

137

after my father, as if he did not exist for them. But then, only The News existed for Dennis; and nobody in town had ever appeared on television.

"Mr. D'Andrea, you won't tell Johnny, will you? About my being with Rand?"

"Honey, everybody knows about Rand. Everybody saw you, if not here, somewhere. Important thing is, you didn't fall. Don't matter how close to the edge you get, long as you pull back. Kids go four years to college and never learn that. Here it is only November and you got it down, right?" He patted my shoulder absently, like my father watching The News.

I managed not to sob until I was with Gretchen, and then we sobbed together.

Thirteen

One week before Thanksgiving.

The temperature had dropped to zero when the tide was out and in spite of being saltwater, the shallows of the tidal flats had frozen. As the tide rose it lifted the slushy salt ice. The surface of the sea looked like gray suede.

I sat in the car, motor running for warmth, and stared at the empty public beach. The handrails of the stone steps had rusted. Icicles hung upside down from it: brown icicles, filled with sand and seaweed.

The tide slowly withdrew, leaving its slush behind. The slush kept the pattern of the waves and lay upon the beach like pizza dough, waiting emptily till the filling returned.

A quarter mile out to sea lay Salt Island, a series of boulders with a ruff of tall grass. The ice had coated the promontory so that it looked like a mound of salt: not sugar, which would be pretty, but salt — heavy, grainy, and sour.

Sea gulls clustered, neither flying nor flapping, but hung like kites on strings, where the air currents mixed to let the birds float as if on water.

Far out to sea a layer of mist coated the water. Some large ship passed slowly by, its lower portions hidden, only its superstructure visible.

Ice washed up.

Slabs piled in on each other however the waves shoveled them, stacked like giant reams of paper needing alignment.

Winter.

So very winter.

In other worlds, friends of mine were cross-legged on unmade beds in messy dorms, trading gossip and textbooks.

My world, my pitiful world, had nothing in it but ice and salt.

I drove away only because I could not drive off the edge. Stone retaining walls prevented me from driving into the sea. I drove among the summer houses, boarded up and grim.

I drove through the marina simply because the car was pointed that way, and I stopped for Mr. D'Andrea only because he was blocking the road.

"Hey, there, Helen!" he said enthusiastically.

I hated him for being pleased with life. "Hello, Mr. D'Andrea."

"Whatcha up to, kid?"

"Not much." I tried to smile to make up for lack

of speech. I have always particularly loathed a bumper sticker that says: LIFE'S A BITCH AND THEN YOU DIE. I was beginning to see how you could feel that way.

"Want a job?"

"A job," I said warily.

"I'm desperate. Park the car and come answer the telephone for me, will you? We're so shorthanded. Everybody's sick or moving to Florida. If we work in the sheds, we got nobody in the office. Please, Helen? Just for today?"

I was not even gracious about it. "Well, all right, but just this once."

"Fine, fine, fine," said Mr. D'Andrea, hustling me into the office. "Phone," he said, pointing, "extension numbers, files, coffee pot. Good luck. See you later."

The office was as cluttered as Vegas's side of the room. There seemed no point even beginning to clean. Just torch the place. It was lucky Mr. D'Andrea had pointed to the phone or I'd have had trouble finding it under the catalogs, newspapers, price lists, junk mail, bank statements, apple cores, and wrappings off fast foods.

The phone rang. Mr. D'Andrea had not told me what to say. Vaguely I recalled a day in elementary school, when I was covered with poison ivy, going with my mother to some office, where Gloria spent the day crisply answering several phones. So, crisply, I said, "Marina." In one millisecond, I ran through name possibilities. Helen Miranda — too long. Miss Revness — doubtful if anybody at the marina used, or even knew, last names. Hallie — another world; some lighthearted happy world from which I had graduated. "Helen here. May I help you?"

"Oh, my God," said a heavy male voice. "Is this the voice of competence? It's about time. Now the place will function. Listen, it's Joe at Hardison's. We're gonna be a day late with the delivery. Not that it matters to you guys. You can't tell one day from another."

I laughed. "Who do I tell that to?"

"Who's there?"

"Nobody."

He laughed with me. "Sounds like that marina. If anybody ever shows up, tell 'em. Bye."

I searched for blank paper on which to write a message. None. I wrote it on an envelope which I stuck in my jeans pocket so it wouldn't get lost in the mess.

There wasn't even a wastebasket to put the apple cores in. The floor required a rake, or possibly a shovel. Finally I cleared enough space to spread a newspaper and used that for a garbage pail. I started with food and used tissues, wishing for gloves. I made bank paper piles, order paper piles, and questionable piles. Slowly the surfaces of three desks emerged. By this time I'd taken five more messages, from Mitch, Rory, Pasquale, June, and Evie. Each about an unidentified object. "He'll know," they all assured me, hanging up.

The office had a bathroom, under whose sink were cleaning materials. Unopened. I scrubbed a desk top, Lysoled the telephone, and put my back-of-the-envelope messages on the now sweet-smelling surface.

The phone rang again. "Marina. Helen here. May I help you?"

"Hallie, I can't believe it," Johnny said. "You sound so experienced already. You must be a clone of your mother. How did Dad talk you into this?"

"He blocked the road. It was either work today or run him down."

"I'm so glad you're here. Listen, Mitch call?"

"Yes. He has twelve hundred."

"Wonderful. Call him back and tell him we'll take them all."

Johnny hung up without telling me Mitch's last name, his company, or twelve hundred what. But I had unearthed a little go-around thing of phone numbers on cards. It would be tedious flipping from A to Z looking for a first name Mitch, but there was nothing else to do. I reached E when it occurred to me that it might actually be under M for Mitch, and sure enough, under M for Mitch was a cryptic listing: HBC and a number. The high priestess of tele-phones, as Flavia used to call me, surfaced mo-mentarily. I called HBC.

"HBC," said the answerer unhelpfully.

"This is Helen at the marina. I need to speak to Mitch about the twelve hundred."

It was like calling Flavia at her dorm. The sweet

143

phone voice switched into its Enough Volume To Reach Mars mode. *"Mitch!"*

"Yo," said Mitch into the phone.

I rolled my eyes at the wall. *Yo?* Was this seventh grade? "Helen at the marina. We'll take all twelve hundred."

"Hey, great. When do you want 'em?"

"Now," I said, having no idea.

"Okay. I'll load 'em. Nice doing business with ya, Helen. Ya got a mind, which nobody else down there features. Ya staying on or ya already disgusted with the general level of brain down there?"

I giggled. "I'm going to try to uplift them."

"Jeez, honey, I hope you got a few decades." He hung up.

You must be a clone of your mother.

It was something I would have to think about.

Somebody had covered the wall with the detailed marine charts so essential for sailing. Thumbtacked over the charts were literally hundreds of old messages and notices, with the faded look of ancient days. Careful folding turned a piece of paper into a bag. Tossing tacks into a desk drawer nobody used (these people were surface storers), I began cleaning the wall. Some papers, glued by time and the sun, didn't even fall when I took out the tack.

"Helen, call in lunch, will you?" said Mr. D'Andrea the next time he phoned. "We want eleven specials from the diner, pick-up in fifteen minutes. You want a special, too, or you want something else? We just take the special. But you order anything you want.

We bring our own drinks, but you order yours, huh?"
He hung up.

I phoned the diner. "Hi, Gale. It's Helen, Gloria Revness's daughter. I'm ordering eleven — no, make that twelve — specials to pick up for the marina in fifteen minutes."

"Helen, I swan. You working down there? How's your mama? What state she in now? When's she coming home? I don't have any fill-in. I'm going crazy, I need that woman."

They liked Gloria so much. She was famous here. Because she'd worked in every building. "They came down California, swept through Nevada and Texas, and now they're doing New Orleans." The postcard collection was from the other end of the Mississippi now. It felt more Mississippi-ish.

"She'll come home thankful," said Gale, firmly as an oracle. "There's no place like home. Course the food might be better in New Orleans." She paused hopefully.

"Gale, could even New Orleans beat your specials?"

"Atta girl, you got possibilities."

The day raced by.

Mr. D'Andrea ran in around three and handed over a pink billing slip on the back of which he had scribbled the names of nine boats. "We got nothing on those boats, Helen. Just their names. They been sold, but we don't know who to. So there they are in the water. We got a major storm coming up, they're gonna swamp, get ripped off their moorings.

145

You see if you can track down their owners, tell them to get up here and save their boats."

"But how do I do that?"

He pointed at files. "If there's an answer, it's in there, but there's probably no answer. People that don't keep in touch, what are we supposed to do, you know what I mean?" He left. It took me an hour to figure out the filing system and get even a remote idea how to track down the ownership of boats for which I had only the boat's name, and not the owner's.

Johnny appeared. "Should I keep any of this?" I asked, pointing to my piles.

Johnny sat on the edge of my scrubbed desk while he made two phone calls. "You decide, Hallie. Nobody here knows."

"Johnny, will you call me Helen, please?" He didn't ask why, for which I was grateful. I didn't know why. But I needed not to be Hallie for a while. Perhaps forever.

He nodded. "You decide, *Helen*. Nobody here knows."

"Is this any way to run a marina? It seems very slapdash to me."

"It's not any way to run a marina and it is slapdash. We do boats, not offices. Place is all screwed up. You just can't get help."

In other contexts (like Sea Storm) "help" meant lower-level hired scum, but here, "help" was a rescue squad.

By five o'clock everybody had gone home except

Mr. D'Andrea. He, too, sat on the edge of the desk. Nobody used chairs; they were for litter.

"Now here's what you have to do," I said, because Mr. D'Andrea seemed ready to leave without finding out what I had accomplished. "You have to return Evie's call; she's still worried. Mitch is delivering all twelve hundred tomorrow. I don't know what Evie's worried about, or what Mitch is delivering. Pasquale says next week is better, so pick a date. There's no calendar here. I marked out squares on a blank piece of paper for today, but you have to order one of those big calendars that fill up the whole desk. Rory wants to know can he put the McWhidden job ahead of the Amory job. Here. I wrote it on one index card so it will fit in your shirt pocket and you can't lose it." I handed it over. "Now, I've figured out how the files work, but I didn't have time to find the owners. I can stay later, and finish that, but I don't want to stay by myself, so you have to stay and make the phone calls with me."

He stared, mouth open like Vegas's, that horrible day in Flavia's dorm. My words filtered back to me. How bossy, how dictatorial! Who was I but some seventeen-year-old Mr. D'Andrea had rescued only a week ago from a stupid hood?

Mr. D'Andrea nodded a few times. Then he said, "Helen, I'm in love."

If he had marital problems, surely the last person —

"With you, kid," said Mr. D'Andrea, laughing. He looked remarkably like Johnny. For a moment I could not be sure who was sitting there; the years between father and son blurred. "I love efficient people. I love people who just start running things, who I don't have to come after with a cattle prod to make 'em work. Want a job?"

Fourteen

I had had no idea how satisfying it would be to make a mess orderly. Even the tasks nobody could tell me how to do, I muddled through. And I hardly needed the phone index. By the second call, I had each number memorized. I was so proud of myself! Several times, when I was alone in the office — first looking out the window to make sure nobody was going to walk in on me — I danced in circles and clapped for myself.

The joy of having high spirits again!

Of being *me*!

Energy bursting forth. Plans for tomorrow!

I hadn't yet telephoned Jaz about the marina job. I wanted to be sure it wasn't a mirage; that it would be as good the second week as the first; that Mr. D'Andrea was not just being friend-ish on account of liking Gloria.

So much to tell Jaz now!

Gary at Supply, Ellen in Welding (yes, Ellen in

Welding), PJ in Sales (yachts), and Katy and Rimmie in Sails (sewing). My telephone buddies: Mitch, who called to flirt; Rory and June, who were already so involved in my life and problems that Rory wanted me to take business courses at night, and June said if Rand Willems reappeared, June's son had a shotgun.

I would tell Jaz how quickly I relearned typing from that rinky little high school course. How it was clear, sorting through the wall notes, that a lot of customers had requested marine charts over the years. How I myself suggested to Mr. D'Andrea that we sell charts so customers don't have to go across town to the hardware and fishing supply store. How he nodded, gave no instructions, but simply said, "Go for it, Helen." How PJ, who is seventy-seven, has retired three times now and is next in line loving me after Mr. D'Andrea. (Johnny says he'll be third in line, which is not a hardship because, he explained, eventually the others will die off and he'll move up to first place.)

I could laugh again.

I had actually missed the sound of my own laughter. Hearing myself laugh was as joyous as hearing other people laugh.

When Jaz said, "What are you up to?" I'd have something to say.

I was no longer jealous of campus life. My days were interesting, too, things to do and people to talk with. The burden of empty hours vanished. There were no hours anyway: just days that flashed by. I even arrived at the marina by eight in the morning. (Willingly; I couldn't wait to tell Jaz, since he had sworn off early classes. "Early?" I would scoff. "I'm up and working before you even find your way out of the dorm, Jaz Innes.")

Come spring, Mr. D'Andrea told me, the office would be filled by a tide of customers, all of whom would want to chew the fat and generally feel at home. "Oh, we give 'em a hard time, tell 'em they're nothing but city people — but they're our kind of people. They sail. They love boats. They love the Atlantic. And we love them. So you'll run an open house, come spring. You'll tell 'em where to buy what, and generally be their buddy. You're like your mom, Helen, you'll be perfect."

I began reading again, for the first time since high school ended, but not the fat historical paperback romances I usually preferred — my mother's cookbooks. It was easy to find Gloria's favorite recipes: the books flipped open to gravy stains or cinnamon sugar.

I called everyone at college, including several from the year before's class, inviting them to a Friday-after-Thanksgiving party. Every single person accepted. Even Susannah, who had sworn not to visit the East Coast till she could buy her own jet and fly it back herself, was coming home. Flavia. Valerie. Michael.

I called Jaz last, savoring it like dessert. I didn't even tuck up on my bed to make the call; I was so full of energy, I called from the kitchen, where there's room to dance. "Jaz, I'm so glad to hear your voice."

"Oh, God, Hallie, don't tell me you're depressed again. I can't stand it. I really can't. Everything here is great, and one call from you and my week is ruined."

The dancing stopped. Almost, my heart with it.

"I'm sorry," he said wearily. "I didn't mean that, Hallie. It's just that I can't even say 'How are you?' because the answer is too depressing."

"Not this time, Jaz. I have good news. I got a wonderful job. At the marina. Running the office."

"The marina?" he repeated. "You mean that attic-y room above the storage shed? Where people get change for the laundromat? What do you mean, *run*? There's nothing there."

"I — yes, there is, Jaz. It's very exciting and I'm making all these friends."

"But Hallie, you didn't want to wait on people at Sea Storm. What's the difference? Come summer, you'll be kowtowing to every yachtie in Maine."

Strange to be Hallie again, after being Helen for so many marina phone calls. Who is Hallie? I thought. Some of her died this fall. I tried to remember what I had been so excited about, telephoning Jaz. "I can wear nice clothes. And that matters, Jaz. I love clothes, I really do. And it's my office. Nobody else wants it."

"Gee," Jaz said, casting around for something to say, anything at all, "that's nice, Hallie. I'm glad you like it. I'm sure it's very . . . um . . . interesting. Well, listen, Hallie, the timing here isn't too good. Rob and Charlie and I — "

"No, wait!" I said, babbling. "I want you to understand, Jaz. A boatyard is complex. Like, well, for example, here's something exciting I came up with myself." I told him about the maps. About how Rimmie and Katy wanted me to learn to sew sails.

"Sewing sails?" Jaz said incredulously. "*Sewing?* Some seamstress in a sweat factory?"

"It's custom work, Jaz. Every sail is different. It's very interesting, how Rimmie and Katy help design the sails." I was getting frantic. "And for lunch," I said desperately, "we all order the special from the diner."

He was silent.

"Jaz, how could you not care about my job? That I've picked myself up? Aren't you glad I learned what to do with this terrible freedom?"

"What's bad about freedom? My whole campus is campaigning for more."

"You can have too much freedom, Jaz. And then it's torture."

"A job clerking in some closed-for-the-winter office is better? I can't figure you out, Hallie."

"I'm a different person now, Jaz. We all are."

"The difference is, you settled for nothing. Hallie, the girls here are — " he sighed again.

"Studying Chinese and geology," I finished.

"I'm more interested in those than sewing," he said.

Don't fight. Let it go. "Jaz, I'm having a reunion

party Thanksgiving weekend. Everybody's coming."

Silence. Did he have other plans? Better things to do? I made the only offering left to me. "You can hear how everybody's doing at college," I said desperately.

"I'll be there," said Jaz.

Emmett was banging a plastic bowling pin against the piano leg. Leighton was running around and around the downstairs pushing a toy lawn mower that popped wooden marbles like a machine gun. It was difficult to imagine why anybody would want children. Easy to imagine why grandparents had decided interstate traffic was better.

"Where are Mom and Dad now, anyway?" grumbled Royce.

"Virginia," hollered Jen. "James River Estates."

"What's that, a housing development?"

"Historic plantations." Jen looked as if she would either like to be touring such a mansion herself, or else drowning the children in the James River, and *then* touring the mansion.

"We can't have Derek for Thanksgiving dinner," I yelled. "Gretchen's coming, and if Derek shows up with some girlfriend, it will be awful."

"Shouldn't Gretchen be over this by now?" said Royce. "It's been a year."

"There's a timetable for recovery?" snapped his wife. "One year later Gretchen's supposed to have fun at a party attended by her husband's girlfriend? If anyone did that to me, I'd commit a homicide."

154

"She means you," I told my brother. "Play around and you're dead meat."

"Speaking of dead meat, who's cooking the turkey?"

It seemed that Gloria had always done that; nobody else knew how. Turkeys were frozen, or something, they took weeks to defrost. Jen actually wanted to telephone all campgrounds in the James River area to ask Gloria how to cook the turkey.

"Please," I said. "I want her to come home. She'll drive through Mexico and fight in Central American revolutions before she comes home, if we bother her about how to defrost a turkey. I'll do the turkey."

Jaz called. "Hallie? I'm sorry, okay? I didn't mean to cut you off and not sympathize and all."

"It's all right, Jaz. I know it's been miserable listening to me all these weeks."

"I'm glad you're feeling better. I bet it's a great job."

"Yes, it is." My heart pounded. But what his heart was doing, I did not know. I said, "Being long distance is so much harder than I thought it would be, Jaz."

"Yes."

"But you'll be here for Thanksgiving," I prompted.

"Yes."

There would be no analysis of where we went wrong; what we yearned for. But he would be here. In person. I would know; I could see and feel. And it would be all right.

We decorated the house with turkeys Meg made in nursery school. Meg's handprint in red paint formed the turkey's body and tail.

Gretchen, who's a wonderful cook, wanted to cook for somebody again. "You do the family Thanksgiving," she offered, "and I'll do your reunion party."

Gretchen was not kidding around. She prepared three dips, seven hors d'oeuvres, a vast pot of chili, layer cakes, and apple pies. She laid in ice cream by the ton, chips by the truck, and enough rolls and roast beef to make an army of sandwiches. "I'm so happy to be a hostess again," Gretchen confided. "I love having parties. One of the awful things about divorce is there's nobody to party with."

I was divorced, too. From high school.

If I had known that marriage would end — the union of Hallie the Prom Queen and Westerly High — would I have lived differently?

People arrived very early.

Brittany, still homesick, was first. We embraced like people saving each other from a sinking ocean liner. "I'm in the home stretch, Hallie. Only three weeks till Christmas vacation."

It was odd to be called Hallie again. That name, light as air, had blown away for good. I was Helen. "It must be awful, Brittany," I sympathized.

She told me in exhaustive detail how awful it was.

I began to have sympathy for Jaz. Had my depression been so boring?

Valerie came. Max. Kyle. Gordon.

By six o'clock (an hour before they were even invited) eighteen had arrived. I shrieked, "I'm so glad to see you!" till my throat was sore. Cheerleader again. I loved it.

I could feel Jaz out there, coming. He'd be pulling in any minute now. My body was waiting, ready to hurl itself Jaz-ward. My heart singing *Jaz, jaz, jaz, jaz, jaz, jaz, jaz.* I have so much to tell you! How to file maps, how to order engine parts, how I'm part Gloria!

Flavia arrived with Vegas. Vegas, who'd said *if this is your best friend, it shows how little there is to pick from.* I was stunned. "Hi," I said. "It's so nice to have you." Though it wasn't.

"It's too far for me to go home for only four days," Vegas said nervously. "Flavia thought it would be okay for me to come to your party."

"Of course it is. Dip's here. Chili's there."

Vegas, not shy, joined Kyle.

"Hi, Flavia," I said. "Welcome home."

"She's my roommate. Don't be mad, Hallie. I had to bring her. If you don't get along with your room-mate, life is the pits."

I could accept that. I knew something about life in the pits. "How've you been?"

Flavia looked worn out. She had circles under her eyes and her hair lacked shine. "Oh, fine. School's a little demanding. I bit off too much this year. I haven't heard from you lately."

We were afraid of each other. "I've been busy," I said carefully. "I have a wonderful job. I'm running the marina office."

Disbelief in her voice. "Johnny D'Andrea's father's marina?" Flavia looked around, to reassure herself that only our old crowd was here. Only the college kids.

I had a stab of guilt. It had never crossed my mind to ask Johnny to this party — and yet he was my only friend. "Right. It's fun. I'm good at it."

In her most neutral voice, she said, "That's nice."

All the lovely marina stories and people, never to be shared with Flavia. No sharing next summer either. I'd be working ten hours a day, seven days a week, June, July, and August. ("But six weeks' vacation whenever you want it between January and April," Mr. D'Andrea had promised.)

"How about some chili, Flavia? Gretchen made it; it's wonderful."

"Oh, how is Gretchen?" Flavia cried, as if she cared; as if she had actually thought about Gretchen from Princeton.

"Gretchen's in the kitchen. Go say hi." Gretchen was surrounded by college kids, attacking her food with such enthusiasm that she was whipping up second batches. Six kids were saying, "Real food. Mommy food. Food with flavor. Food with texture. Who are you? We love you. Would you come back to college with us?" Gretchen laughed and flushed and was happy.

I went back into the living room. Jaz, I thought, jaz, jaz, jaz, jaz, jaz.

But it was Michael who arrived next.

"I wasn't sure you'd come," I cried, hugging him. "I'm so glad to see you. Is it going to bother you that Flavia's here?"

Michael grinned. "I'm pretty darn glad to see you, too, Hallie. No, it isn't going to bother me. Flavia was absolutely right. The first week on campus . . ." He paused and looked at me sideways. "I met this girl."

I love sentences like that. I twinkled back at him. "And?"

"And we're engaged."

I practically dropped the chili bowl.

"Her name is Marielle," Michael said reverently.

"Michael, congratulations, that's so exciting. Do you have a photograph of Marielle?"

"Of course," he said, as if I'd asked if he had toes. Gordon and Kyle came up to punch him. They yelled each other's names, yelled How *are* you? Good to *see* you! and the college talk began.

College courses.

College curriculum requirements.

College costs.

College telephone bills.

College exams, soon to begin.

I passed hors d'oeuvres. Invited everybody to

make roast beef sandwiches. Everybody did. Offered seconds on chili. Everybody had some.

"You think your roommate's bad. Wait till you hear about mine."

"Listen, I'm already on my third roommate."

"That's nothing, we're on our third RA, our floor is so rotten."

"What's an RA?" I asked.

Eyes swiveled like cats in the dark. Remembering that Hallie did not go to college.

"An RA," Vegas said gently, "is a Resident Advisor. A senior class person who is both floor supervisor and confidant. He or she lives in a single room, centrally located, and is always on call."

I hate you. I am seriously considering drowning you. But I want it to hurt. Maybe I'll slice you. Like a turkey.

"Well put," said Kyle. "You must be taking Public Speaking."

"No. I'm just naturally very articulate."

Everybody howled with laughter.

"What's that racket?" Flavia demanded suddenly. "Who has a radio on so loud?"

"It's a trumpet," Michael said, who had been in Band for years. "Who could be playing at this hour?"

Michael and Flavia leaned out the window, pressing noses against the dark glass and frowning. It was like old times, seeing them do the same thing at the same moment, but neither Michael nor Flavia noticed.

"Somebody on the sidewalk," Michael said.

160

We flung open the door.

A trumpeter played a fanfare, brilliant and gaudy, like kings in the Middle Ages. Into the frigid November air, the kids poured.

Jaz.

Red roses in his hand. A trumpeter at his back. "I didn't," he explained, "want to make my entrance unnoticed."

So gloriously familiar! All my old high school friends, in their beloved postures. Jaz, lying on the floor, laughing without sound. Michael, leaning against the wall, turning now and then to add a log to the fire. Flavia, full of stories. Susannah topping them. (California topped everything.) "I," Susannah explained, "have lived through an earthquake. So there."

"We all lived through an earthquake," I said. My life had convulsed and left me at the bottom of the crack. But I'm on top of the world now, I thought. Noise, friends, music, talk, food, and laughter. What better combination? This'll be a tradition. We'll always gather here. Whenever they think of home, they'll think of me. I'll be the anchor; each fall they'll think about Thanksgiving and get excited about seeing everybody again. At my party.

Jaz nuzzled the back of my neck, looping the thick braid around his wrist. Trumpets and roses! Only Jaz.

"But don't you think," Flavia said, "that the administration is remiss in allowing that sort of activity?"

"Certainly not!" cried Susannah. "What business is it of the administration how we conduct our lives? We're old enough to vote and die for our country!"

Jaz sat up. "But surely, there is some responsibility."

"I had Philosophy 101," Kyle said, "and we discussed — "

"Philosophy," Flavia said in disgust. "Ancient outdated junk they expect you to spew back. This is now. This is AIDS, and crack, and every other addiction. This is homelessness and child abuse and greed."

"That's true," Jaz said. "Other generations didn't have to deal with that." He shifted closer to Flavia and the center of the discussion.

"Isn't it like a time warp, coming back here?" Susannah said. "This is such a backwater. Doesn't it make you laugh, that you used to fit in?"

"When I think how juvenile we were! The opinions we thought were intelligent!"

"And how we used to spend our time," put in Flavia. "Think of the hours we wasted. We could have skipped senior year and not missed a thing. I forgot to bring my high school yearbook to Princeton but I was glad. People who kept harking back to high school were so pitiful."

"I forgot about senior year," Jaz said.

"How many hours a night do you study?" Flavia asked.

"I never study, I just listen in class."

"I study Monday through Thursday. Weekends I party."

"My campus is fabulous for parties! Dorm parties, frat parties, beer parties, street parties!"

"Yeah, but are you going to flunk out?"

I was the maid. Gathered plastic cups. Gave out forks for pie. Remembered who wanted it à la mode. I hated doing this at Sea Storm for wintertime summer people. I hated even more doing it for my friends. "Aren't you glad to be home, though?" I asked them. Like a duck, waddling up hoping for a crust of bread.

"Absolutely! What a relief to get away from the dorm for a while. You just can't imagine the pressure we're under, Hallie. No privacy and next door to the weirdest individuals in history. My college is supposed to have admissions standards and you should see the animals on my floor. We call it True Zoo."

Jaz grinned. "We call our floor The Great American Stud Factory." He fell against Susannah, laughing, and Flavia leaned forward to rub noses with him. "Then how come they let you live there, Jaz?"

No party had ever been a greater success.

I knew because when they left, each guest told me so. "I had the best time!" they cried. "I caught up on what everybody's doing at college."

Flavia's hug was quick and efficient. "Vegas has never seen the East Coast and we're hitting Boston tomorrow, New York on Sunday."

No time with Flavia? My best friend? No time to explain, make her see? A campus was worth visiting. A marina office was not. I held her coat sleeve, swallowing.

"Thanks for a wonderful party," Flavia said.

"Thank you for having me," Vegas said.

"It was a pleasure," I lied.

Are all parties like this? Do you lie like mad at the end of them? Or is Life the party where you lie like mad at the end?

This was Thanksgiving, on which I had staked my life. I was alone with Jaz at last; we would put it back together.

I would be Hallie the cheerleader again; the boundless energy, the scheduling, the laughter, the kissing.

I even thought of the night: me alone in the house with plenty of bedrooms. Jaz alone with me, Jaz who had stayed away from girls for my sake all these weeks.

I turned my face up to his, remembering the exact tilt of the nine inches between us.

He said nervously, "Can't believe how fast the semester has flown by, can you?"

"I don't have a semester," I reminded him. *Put your arms around me, Jaz! Love me. Snuggle me.* Tell me you haven't forgotten senior year!

"Oh, right. I keep forgetting the entire world doesn't live at college." He grinned awkwardly and jammed his hands in his pockets. The hands that had once spent their entire existence touching me.

He poked at some embers in the dying fire with his shoe. "Well, listen," he said. "This — this was the best party."

My head filled with fog.

Jaz wet his lips. He studied the party debris. "Hallie, I'm — I'm sorry. It isn't there anymore. I mean — us." He blew enough air out of his lungs to fill several balloons. "College is so absorbing. Maybe if you were there . . . but you're not. I haven't dated anyone; I promise I haven't. And I don't have anybody in mind either, but I sort of understand what Flavia did when she — um — stopped seeing Michael. You make such good new friends at college, and it's hard . . . uh . . ."

I linked my fingers together. Thought about the jade necklace I had never worn, not once. Of his class ring on the silver chain, which I had never taken off, not once.

He looked miserable. For a moment I thought he would be the one to cry. I wanted him to. I wanted to hit him and give him black eyes. "Do you want to stay friends, Jaz?"

"Oh God, Hallie! We are friends! Good friends. We're just not — "

I didn't want him to break the swear diet now, of all times. "Best friends," I supplied.

He studied the molding around the fireplace, as if planning to build a reproduction once he got back to Ann Arbor. "I thought I could fanfare us back together," he said. "The trumpet — I don't know.

The roses. I thought — but Hallie, it was just a gimmick. Maybe all the things we did in high school were just gimmicks."

Don't say that. Leave memories anyway. My senior year was perfect, even if you've forgotten yours.

I took the silver chain off. It was long. I didn't need to undo the catch. I handed it to him. He stared at the chain. He had forgotten it. I could not bear any more proof of how much more interesting college was than senior year. Than me. *Leave now, Jaz. Drive away.*

"Thanks for being a good sport," he said. "I — I'll miss you."

Did people normally break up this quickly? In five minutes? Impossible; everybody would be in the street with a suitcase. But perhaps it had not been fast; perhaps we had been breaking up all semester.

Like Gretchen at Derek, I flung myself at Jaz one more time. "What days will you be home over Christmas? We could get together." I was pitiful, like Marcy.

"We're going skiing in Canada over Christmas holidays. I won't be in Maine at all." He came close, as if to kiss, but from Jaz, I never wanted a friendish kiss.

I opened the door. Frigid gusts bit our faces. "Bye, Jaz. Take care of yourself."

He left.

I shut the door. Leaned on it. Listened to his boots on the ice. Listened when the engine caught. Listened to his Jaguar drive away without me. Without Morse code.

And the horrible whisper of the whole horrible autumn came back. *Now what? now what? now what?* With its horrible answer, *Now nothing, now nothing, now nothing.*

Fifteen

So that was Thanksgiving.

I gave thanks, at least, for an office to go to on Monday, so I couldn't stay at home and cry.

Jaz called me at work.

I had a customer on one extension arguing about the charges for fixing his two outboards, a customer on another extension deciding he could not afford the boat he had just bought, and a desperate boat owner who had not asked to have his boat stored for the winter asking to have it done that day.

Jaz said, "I just wanted to make sure you're okay. I feel rotten about the whole thing, the way I handled it. We need to talk."

"Jaz, I'm not at college. I'm not between classes. I'm at work."

"I know, but this is pretty important."

I put him on Hold. Solved the billing problem, took a deep breath, and came back to Jaz.

"I didn't expect college to have such an effect, I guess," Jaz said.

"It's been a jolt," I agreed.

Johnny walked in. I reached for a Kleenex, pretending to have a cold.

"Talk to me!" Jaz said.

"I can't. I'm at work. Thanks for worrying." In front of Johnny, I could not say Jaz's name. Could not say anything. "I'll survive. Good-bye." I disconnected, got Johnny the repair record he needed, and spent fifteen minutes pretending to straighten old files, while my tears fell into the bottom of the drawer.

My parents called next.

"I'm sorry to bother you at work," Gloria said, "but I wanted to know how the reunion party went. We haven't been able to get you at home."

I considered telling the truth, but what I learned my own first semester is, Lie a lot. "Great. Forty-two came. Gretchen had such fun cooking that she's going to start her own catering service. Isn't that wonderful? And she can stay home with Meg more. She's breaking into catering by cooking at Sea Storm. And today's the start of my third full week."

"I'm so proud of you," said Gloria.

You know so little of me.

The phone calls were torture. June and Mitch and Rory and Pasquale wanted to know how the college kid party had gone. "Very collegiate," I told them.

"Is that good or bad?" asked Mitch.

"Well, it isn't me," I said, and I hung up without saying good-bye, without doing anything except bursting into tears.

It was now officially Christmas season. Sable Mall would have wonderful Christmas decorations. Last year's theme had been icicles; even the tree in the center of the mall was carved of real ice. But I'd have to go alone. Where, oh where, was a friend?

A present came in the mail from Jaz, so quickly that he must have bought it before Thanksgiving. "I'm still thinking of you," he wrote on the card. "I'll always think of you." It was a music box: a tiny cherry piano with a tiny green wreath looped around its little music ledge. It played "Silent Night."

"I don't want a Silent Night!" I screamed out loud in the empty house. I crushed the wrapping paper with my fists and hurled the ball against the wall. It hit soundlessly and fell to the floor behind some furniture. "I want a Party Night! What am I to do with a life made up of Silent Nights?"

Johnny sat on my desk using the phone to argue about a mixed-up shipment. "Nice Thanksgiving?" he asked me when he hung up.

Thanksgiving seemed an eternity ago. "Yes."

"I love a small town and a big family, don't you?" Johnny said. "It always amazes me that so many people move away and never come back. I don't know what's out there that they want."

"Me neither. And I've certainly listened to enough

170

explanations of it." I found myself telling Johnny about the Thanksgiving party, about Jaz, and the music box. "I don't want to get an MBA like Flavia, or speak Chinese like Jaz. But I don't want Silent Nights. I want Party Nights."

"Party with us."

"You're just being kind. I hate kindness."

"This is the season."

"It's the season for being kind to others, but there's never a good season to receive kindness. That's how you know you're a failure. When people are friend-ish. I miss having a girlfriend. I miss Flavia so much! I miss high school!"

Johnny was interested, but puzzled. "I hated high school. A lot of us did. It just went on and on. People like you and Flavia thrived, but we could never figure out why."

"People like Flavia can't figure it out anymore either. They keep saying they've forgotten senior year." Memory sat in my lap like a puppy wanting attention. I started crying. "Even Jaz," I said.

I truly have nothing now, I thought. Even pride. Look at me sobbing in front of Johnny D'Andrea.

Johnny made no move to comfort me. "I'm sorry," he said finally. "I remember how proud you were of being Class Couple."

I pretended to add up figures. I knew he knew there weren't any figures to add.

The phone rang. I called on God for strength to speak coherently. I had stopped using the word entirely in my swear diet. Perhaps it could have a use, however. "Marina. This is Helen. May I help you?" Come on, God, help me help me help me not collapse.

"Hi, Ed Vannemann here. I wondered if you'd found somebody yet."

"Ed Vannemann," I repeated, raising eyebrows at Johnny. "Have we found somebody yet. Let me see . . ."

Johnny made a face and took the phone. "Hi, Mr. Vannemann, Johnny D'Andrea. We haven't turned anybody up. Remember we said you'd have better luck with a real estate agent." Johnny drummed his fingers in a pattern on the desk. I imitated him. Our fingers became attacking spiders. "I know, Mr. Vannemann. A realtor is apt to bring just anybody in and you don't want a stranger, but nobody's looking for winter housing." His fingers caught mine.

"What do you mean, winter housing?" I said.

Johnny covered the phone with his palm. "You know the condos over the cliffs? He's in the first one. Fabulous view. Owns that ninety-foot yacht we're so behind on. It's seagoing. His crew is taking it to the Aegean so he can sail in the Greek Isles this winter. Not bad, huh?" He took his hand off the phone. "I realize you're not charging rent, Mr. Vannemann, you'd pay somebody to live there, but nobody turned up that we could recommend."

I took the phone out of Johnny's hand.

"Mr. Vannemann? I'd like to be your tenant."

* * *

The condo had six rooms on five levels. So much space was taken up by stairs and balconies there was hardly any left for furniture, so it was built in: pews of couches, strewn with colorful pillows, faced so much glass that the room had a baked look: tanned by the sun. It was a world-class view.

Mr. Vannemann said if the D'Andreas recommended Helen Miranda Revness, that was good enough for him. He said he'd be in Europe for a while. A break in Egypt. Then friends in Dallas. Probably not back here till August. Probably stay a couple of weeks then. Wanted somebody to occupy the place. Water the plants.

"It seems more reasonable to buy new plants each year," I said to Johnny.

Johnny laughed. He went with me to inspect the condo.

White nubbly rugs and a telescope for watching the sea. My own place, close enough to walk to the marina.

When we got back to work, Mr. D'Andrea congratulated me. Gary said it was a big step, real big. PJ said when was I inviting him to spend the night? Katy and Rimmie said when was I going to start sewing sails?

"What does that have to do with getting my first house?"

"Nothing, but we have to make a pitch whenever we can. We're desperate. Even if we sew around the clock till June we won't fill all the special orders."

Somebody needs me, I thought. Not Jaz. Not Flavia. I guess you take what you can get in this world. "Okay. After I get moved in."

Katy and Rimmie promised to move my stuff in fifteen minutes flat.

"You know what comes next, Helen Miranda?" Johnny said. His eyes were twinkling and his cheeks rosy, like Santa. He was so handsome. And I kind of liked it that he was only two inches taller; it made us more equal; I didn't feel I was begging for his attention, the way I had that horrible last five minutes of my life with Jaz. "What? You're only number three, you know, Johnny."

"The minute a person has her own apartment, do you know what comes next?"

"What?"

"A car. You gotta buy a car, lady. You're earning money now. You have free rent. You just got a second job. It's car time. Start test driving."

"A car." I breathed. Breathed again, as if testing my lungs. *"Of my own?* Oh wow, Mr. D'Andrea, can I afford it? Are you paying me that much?"

Mr. D'Andrea declined to get involved in my budget.

Car images planted themselves all over the room. "Or maybe a truck," I said thoughtfully. "I love pickups. You're so nice and high up off the road. Maybe a nice small imported truck."

"Buy American," said PJ firmly, "or I'm off the list."

"Buy foreign," said Johnny. "That moves me up one."

174

* * *

After work, Johnny said, "Would you like to go to the Sand Bar? I usually meet Marcy, Laurie, Billy, and a bunch of others there. It's fun. They have a little dance floor."

I said, "Marcy isn't too fond of me."

He grinned. "No. Well, I'll stand between you if necessary. Come on, Hallie. I mean, Helen. Who else is there?"

"Think you should telephone them first, and tell them to get out their friend-ish-ness?"

"Helen, everybody likes you. You're kind of bossy, but you kind of bit the dust, too. They'll sympathize." He took my hand gently. Like a nursery school teacher.

People I had despised felt sorry for me. People I had ignored would make space for me. People I never dreamed of inviting to my reunion party would party with me. "There's nothing more heartwarming than the Fall of the Wiseass Senior, is there, Johnny?"

"Hey, what happened to the swear diet?"

"That's not a swear word."

"You've slipped, Helen. Come on, set standards for the rest of us."

We drove in his truck. One handsome nice guy teasing me as he drives me to a party should lift my spirits to the heavens. All it made me feel was sad.

High school, O, high school. Come back.

Sixteen

"I'm proud of you," my mother said. "You've handled more in four months than those other kids
will handle in four years." My parents had arrived
home December twenty-first, and in Hurricane Gloria fashion, unpacked, bought a tree, decorated, had
the family for Christmas Day, gave themselves a
welcome home party, and Gloria had a job already.

"That's what Mr. D'Andrea said. But Mother, they
were so awful."

"They're going through a stage," Gloria said.
"They're proud of college. They want to boast. By
next year it won't be so maddening. It's a freshman
syndrome."

Daddy was watching The News. He had not
changed at all. Gloria was not, however, exercising.
In fact, she had put on a little weight. She looked
almost maternal. She had less energy, which in her
case, made her infinitely easier to be near. Did she

go through an earthquake, too? I wondered. And got past it?

"College kids aren't doing anything like as much as I am, Mother. They're still coddled. I got thrown to the wolves!"

My mother lifted the basket of postcards she had sent: North Dakota, Arizona, Maryland. "I could take the easy way out, Helen Miranda, and tell you I did the best I could for you. But I didn't do my best. I got tired. And you're right. I threw you to the wolves. I'm sorry that the wolves turned out to be Flavia and Jaz."

From the living room, the voices of my father's gods intoned their financial liturgies. He still worshipped The News. But Gretchen no longer worshipped Derek; catering siphoned off some of that. And my mother did not appear to worship Fitness.

And who had I worshipped? Jaz? High school? Romance? Or (sick thought; made worshipping The News or Fitness seem positively sane) did I worship Myself as Class Centerpiece?

Gloria began making coffee. Then gave up, as if nothing mattered. She leaned against the gold counter.

How superior my narrow white kitchen in the condo, with its sleek counter and view of the sea, seemed to Mom's big avocado and gold conglomeration of oversized appliances and tiny windows.

"I'm sorry," my mother said. She held out her palms, as if reading the past, not the future. Then she pressed them down hard against the counter, curled them into knots, and went back to making coffee. "I'm truly sorry."

"It's okay, Mother. I'm not mad. Not at you, or any of them. I just feel tired."

"Depression. Cabin fever."

"No. I miss Jaz. Oh, Mommy, I miss Jaz!"

I wept, arms slowly circling my mother, head snuggling against my mother's cheek, and Gloria slowly, unbelievably, began to rock me. Not for muscle tone, but comfort. "Mommy, what am I going to do?"

"What you told him you would. Survive."

"That's fine if you've fallen out of a plane into the Canadian wilderness and have nothing but a knife and your wits. Then survival is terrific. But I'm here, I have everything, from hamburgers to electric blankets. I don't want plain old survival."

Gloria nodded. "You want somebody to love. Somebody to party with."

"Somebody to drive the car, so I can look out the window and choose the radio station."

"Somebody to talk on the phone with."

"Somebody *male*."

We stopped crying. Dried tears. Went to Sable Mall to take advantage of the post-Christmas sales. A tinny song kept bringing us good tidings. Tidings is such a Christmas word. You never use it except at Christmas. Bring me tidings of love, too, I prayed.

We admired a manger scene. I always wanted a lamb. Not sheep. They're dirty. But lambs are pure.

I could use a little purity, flung out on the hillside like white lace handkerchiefs. Of course, I have no hillside. But I have balconies.

I bought three flat wooden lambs with white fleece and black noses. Jaz would be sickened at my lack of good taste. He would say it was no different from sticking a gnome or a toadstool in your yard.

I fastened the lambs to the railings of the outside balconies of the condo. They gamboled above the ocean cliffs. I liked them. "Want to see my office?" I asked my mother shyly.

"Sure. There's nothing like an office, is there? I love setting one up and getting the place regimented so it works efficiently. Then when it's in perfect order, I say, What a bore — now what? So I find another job."

We drove in my new truck.

"I can't get over it," Gloria said. "Your own job, your own place, your own car payments. I am so proud." She admired the dashboard and accessories. "You did it alone, honey, and that's really something. College is hard; there is pressure, although it's a different kind. But you don't do college alone; it's set up to save you from ever being alone. I salute you."

I'm not like Flavia. I don't want to emulate Eleanor Roosevelt, women lawyers, or television anchors. I want to be what I've been: Gloria's daughter. I wanted to say, "You're my role model; I'm going to be you," but I didn't. She might feel threatened. I didn't know her very well. What made Gloria give second-best to mothering, and first-best to jobs? I didn't know what put Gloria into the driver's seat and made her drive west, west, west. But we'd always live in this town. Maybe I'd get to know her better.

"Now getting back to the man problem," Gloria said. "Most sailors are male. Everyone that comes into the office, check him out. See if he needs somebody to crew. Or if they ask you to recommend a restaurant, you could say you just happen to be going there yourself."

"What if they're seventy-three, like PJ?"

"Then they have sons. Or grandsons."

"Mother?"

"What, honey?"

"I still want Jaz."

"He'll be hard to top."

"I don't want to top him. I want to have him."

"Maybe next summer," said my mother. "Time ruined you, honey. Time apart, time doing different things. But he'll be back. Listen, I've seen something of the world now, and here's what I learned. It's all wonderful. There's so much beauty out there. So many great people. But who cares? Home is where your family is. So, once the splendor of college has worn off," Gloria said, "Jaz will be back to what he was."

But Jaz did not have our sort of family. Jaz's family could and did transfer itself without thought; there were no ex-sisters-in-law, or children in nursery school to keep Jaz in one place. Spending a winter on the ocean had been like my parents' trip west, a temporary adventure for the Innes family.

And I was a temporary girl.

I had to sit at the stop sign, blinking, until I could see through my tears and drive on.

"What about Johnny?" my mother said. "He's adorable."

"I can't argue with that. He sort of adopted me, too."

"Brotherly, you mean? That's not good. No romance in that."

"Mom, it's so awful. They're being nice to me. Remember how you used to yell at Flavia and me for not being nice to the creeps who attached themselves to us?"

"Johnny thinks you're a creep? I'll shoot him."

"No, Mom. He feels sorry for me. I absolutely cannot stand people feeling sorry for me. I like the top, not the bottom. I didn't know high school would be the top."

She nodded. "You have a long climb. It won't be easy to set up such a nice life again. But eventually you'll have a good time."

"Mom. New Year's Eve is tomorrow. I don't have a date. I'll sit in front of a TV watching people in Times Square. Tell me how that is a good time."

New Year's Eve, Leighton, Emmett, and Meg were delivered for baby-sitting. The condo had been stripped for the occasion. I was not going to have

Mr. Vannemann sorry he let me house-sit.

"I like your lamb, Aunt Helen," cried Emmett.

"Thank you, Em. I like my lamb, too."

"Is he okay in the snow?"

"He's okay in the snow."

"I want to have a lamb for Christmas, too."

"Christmas is all gone."

Emmett began sobbing. "I want it back!" he yelled.

I knew what he meant. Let's all pick a year and keep it. The hell with new ones.

Emmett began a tantrum. Little children are so wise. They know what matters. Last year matters.

"Helen," said Jen, "sure you don't mind baby-sitting for the whole crew? It's a lot to ask, taking care of all three. They'll never sleep. They're wired."

"It's all right. I like playing with them."

My parents were at the Elks Club. Royce and Jen were going to the New Year's celebration at Sea Storm. Gretchen was working at Sea Storm, and Derek had taken his girl to Mount Snow.

"Do we have to go to bed now, Aunt Helen?" Meg said anxiously.

"No. We're going to stay up till midnight."

Three awestruck faces stared at their Aunt Helen. It sobered them, to think such a thing. They held my hand, as if this meant a journey.

We crawled, butted heads, tickled, chased. Had snacks and a Once upon a time story. The babies fell asleep long before midnight. Emmett lasted longest. "Not sleepy, Aunt Helen," he said, until he tipped over at eleven. It was a good thing he was so short. He had less distance to fall.

The floor was too cold. I scooped each one up, carried them gently to the king-sized bed in the biggest bedroom, and blanketed them heavily.

Then I wrapped myself in a blanket and watched the television. Thank God for television. It's your friend when nobody else is.

Jaz and his parents were skiing in Canada.

Flavia had not come home. Her parents went to New Jersey for a two-day visit, and then Flavia flew to Nevada to stay with Vegas. Susannah stayed in California, getting an apartment with friends. Michael, whose friendship with Jaz remained intact, joined the Inneses in Canada.

Jaz had written me more in the last month than he had the whole rest of the time in college. He kept justifying himself, giving reasons for breaking up. I couldn't stand the letters. What could be worse than being told twenty different ways why you aren't wanted?

At one A.M. the door opened. It was Royce — with Johnny D'Andrea behind him.

"Sis, why didn't you tell us about the party at the marina?" Royce said. "I'll take the kids on home. You go have fun."

I didn't want to move. It was safe, in my blanket cocoon. Fun? With all those friend-ish people?

"Come on," pleaded Johnny. "It's no fun without you. PJ and Gary and Katy and Rimmie and everybody is asking for you. A bunch of people who worked for us last summer are here, and their wives and girlfriends. Bunch of customers who get up every New Year's. The band's still there. Come on." He held out his hand.

We'd decorated one of the metal barns. I'd ordered the decorations, supervised some of the work. "I'm not in a party mood."

"Come on," said Johnny. And in a soft teasing voice, added, "It's special. You'll see."

Special. But there was only one special person in my life.

Jaz.

How like him! From Morse code signals to a trumpet fanfare — Jaz! He missed me. He couldn't usher in a New Year without me. He's here. He sent Johnny to get me.

My heart escaped and ran ahead, down the road, among the boats. "I'm not dressed." I had to look wonderful, had to look Party, had to —

"You have clothes on, don't you? Shoes, don't you? That's dressed. Come on." Johnny had one of the big marina trucks. I could barely step up so high. He put his hands around my waist and boosted me in. It was a frigid night. The stars shivered with cold, looking so tiny they might have shrunk from below-zero temperatures.

Jaz! jaz, jaz, jaz, jaz, jaz.

But of course Jaz wasn't there.

He was skiing in Canada.

PJ had the first dance; Mr. D'Andrea the second.

Johnny was dancing with Marcy and didn't take the third. I danced with Rimmie's husband, Chuck, and then with Mitch, of telephone acquaintance, who it turned out, had graduated with Royce.

Laurie Copp was there, and a dozen other kids from my class. Kids I had forgotten about. Kids I'd considered forgettable. Kids whose photos I didn't use in the candid section of the yearbook because they weren't my friends.

We danced, danced, danced. I danced whether I had a partner or not; whether there was music or not.

Somewhere around three A.M., Marcy said to me, "You know, you're not so bad, Helen."

I kept dancing. I thought if I stopped dancing, I'd start crying. I could not, would not, bring in the New Year with tears.

Johnny and I danced a slow dance, and the tears came anyway. He was wearing a very thick navy blue sweater, with soft cables knit in. "My sweater's braided like your hair," he said. I leaned against his shoulder and let his sweater sop up my tears. He noticed, but said nothing.

I appreciated that. I could not stand any more words of comfort.

"What's the special part of the dance, Johnny?" I said at last.

He did not know what I meant.

"When you picked me up, you said the dance is special."

"Oh. Well, it is, isn't it? I love a party. Don't you?"

At five in the morning, everybody wanted breakfast. "My place," I suggested. "Just don't wear your shoes inside. Mr. Vannemann has white carpet. Socks only."

Marcy said, "I'm good with eggs and toast. I'll short order."

There were nine of us left. Marcy cooked, Johnny made coffee, while Laurie Copp and her boyfriend did a lip-sync routine. One by one, like Leighton, Emmett, and Meg, they surrendered to sleep. Johnny slept on one of the pew-couches. Marcy curled up in the huge recliner that faced the ocean. The condo was thick and breathy with the sounds of their sleep. The coffee smell lingered.

The rising sun was blinding yellow gold.

It was not warm. But it was the promise of warmth.

I thought, I'm thankful again. I have a roomful of friends. A mother who wants to know me better. Nephews and a niece to watch grow up. I could use a girlfriend. I could really use a boyfriend.

Johnny's sleepy voice said, "You okay, Helen?" He got to his feet, wrapped toga style in his blanket. He wound it around me, too, and we watched the sun on the water. "God, it's a beautiful world," he breathed. Then he looked at me. "Sorry. Swear diet."

"It is a beautiful world. Lonelier than I expected, though." I pressed my cheek against the glass. Icy cold.

"Remember hide-and-seek?" Johnny said.

"Sure."

"I always found you."

"I didn't hide very hard."

"Same old forsythia bush."

"Same old Johnny."

He kissed my glass-chilled cheek. I did not analyze the kiss. Brother, co-worker, neighbor, rescuer. It was a kiss. It started my New Year. I'd take it.

"I'm freezing," muttered Marcy. "Are there more blankets?"

"I'll get you one." I went into the bedroom. The red reminder light on my answering machine flickered. I played the tape. It was Jaz. "Hi, Hallie. I'm sorry I missed you. I guess you're out partying. I'm glad. I wanted to wish you a Happy New Year. I. Um. Well." (Answering machines record all scattered thinking.) "Well, Happy New Year, Hallie. Um. Bye."

I wish you a happy New Year, too, Jaz. I hope next time we meet, I won't want to kill you or kiss you, just wave and be old friends. I never knew high school would end, Jaz. I never knew anything would end. But everything did. I just have to trust that other things begin.

"Hey, Helen!" Johnny yelled. "You got any guts? Marcy wants to celebrate New Year's Day wading in the surf."

I erased the tape. I even laughed. Because I learned one thing for sure during my first semester: not geology, not Chinese. But this:

I have guts.

About the Author

CAROLINE B. COONEY lives in a small seacoast village in Connecticut, with three children and two pianos. She writes every day on a word processor and then goes for a long walk down the beach to figure out what she's going to write the following day. She's written about forty books for young people, including *Saturday Night, Last Dance,* and *Summer Nights.*